Second Chance

felix chance volume two
j.e. pittman

For those lost along the way,

and those we nearly did.

Her Name Was Love

Cosmic clock winds forward. Ever forward, never back.

New legends rise for an age — trials, dire, and struggle.

Cosmic clock grinds. Grinds the bones of those who were and would be.

Legends, born again, who never asked — those who do, unworthy.

Cosmic clock grinds, gears stripping.

Hands moving…

Back — the benediction of time.

Her name was love. She was my everything.

How could I forget?

The bliss, the pain, the sheer depth of feeling she evoked. Every life I saw her soul, we danced.

Sunbeams in her hair, playing across her skin and catching in her clear crystal eyes.

Her passion and fierce countenance overwhelming, like a sea frothed in storm. Drowning in her smile.

I'm going under again.

…

..

.

They were not gods — mere pretenders.

The Problem
with Christmas

EVERYONE KEEPS ASKING IF I'm okay. Truth is, I'm not, but I don't know what to say. So I lie.

I put on the brave, bright face people have come to expect from me, because they'd honestly rather be lied to than face a hard truth. I lie about my thoughts, my feelings, my pain. About my name, about my predilections, my past, my potential futures, or their seeming lack. Everything is a lie now. As natural as breathing.

What can I say? I learned from the best. Felix tells lies he doesn't even know are lies.

I asked him once a while back — one of our long car conversations — how I could trust such a consummate liar.

"I've lied to you, true, but I never deceived you," Felix said in the passing shadow of streetlights. Oddly, I believed him.

I lie, even to him. He knows I'm lying, but he doesn't call me on it. I wish he would.

I tell him that I'm okay. That it's not his fault — which it isn't, ultimately, but he certainly bears the burden whether I want him to or not. That I'm still human.

That one's a doozy I even tell myself, trying to deny the changes after that little soul sucker stole more than a kiss. I was stupid, sure, but she broke the pact. I only half believe it happened, dazed as I was. I don't really know what'll happen to me now, but what's scarier is neither does Felix.

So he dumped me. Dumped me in this bar I now apparently own full of lost souls and the wayward damned and went off galavanting on his own. Without me. Exactly what he promised me he *wouldn't* do after Vegas.

Any luck? I'd texted him the week before. This had followed: *This is super creepy!* accompanied by a video of hyper-realistic masks of people-faces. *An old friend of yours dropped by.* And a litany of others that had gone unread.

I miss you, I swiped out, briefly wondering what fun he was off having — again, *without* me — or if he was stuck in the twist when the bathroom exploded.

"Mistress Molly!" Evette insisted on calling me that. Now, rather urgently as I heard a spray of water gushing in the gents. The force of it all rumbled the floors and rattled the pipes. But there was more; hidden in the clatter was a familiar noise I just couldn't place.

Through the door, chaos reigned in comedic tableau. I was reminded of an old sitcom. Fairly standard set piece. Bathroom destroyed, plumbing spraying water from every elbow joint. More pipes bursting. In this episode, one of the two toilets lay shattered on the floor, a dent in the ceiling above. The other had become a bidet. Classic. And as always, one character was frantically rushing from leak to leak, trying in vain to staunch the flow of water — in this instance, a very wet Evette.

The poor soul was soaked, slipping and sliding on the floor as I waded in to help.

"Well," I surveyed the damage, "I wanted to redecorate anyway."

"Mistress, wait!" Evette tried to stop me, spitting water as she held a towel over a spraying main. "It's loose!"

"*What's* loose?" I stopped, looking around the flooding room for whatever had scared Evette. I sloshed to the stalls where the bidet toilet rumbled, shaking violently before it too geysered into the ceiling. A rush of whitewater shot at me, making a sound like a...garbage disposal?

"Look out, Mistress!" Evette dove in front of the wicked beak coming for my face, tangling herself in the furry white long body. In her terror, she tried to throttle the poor creature.

"Don't hurt him, Evette!" I slogged down next to the writhing pair on the slick tile. "Tony!" I snapped, placing my hand on his furry, wet scruff. "Not yours."

The not-so-baby rokuichi stiffened. Evette did, too, eyes flickering to me for guidance yet not leaving the perceived threat long.

"Tonyyyy," drawing it out, not quite middle naming him yet. "Not. Yours."

Sad disposal noises. He released my bartender, curling up around a broken main, trying to hide.

"Mistress?" Evette coughed, hesitantly getting to her feet. I ignored her.

"Tony," I said evenly. He poked his beak out. "I'm not mad at you, Tony, c'mere baby." I held out my arms for the fluff flying my way. "Aww, there there." I scratched him under his sharp beak. Happy disposal noises.

In the tumult, I'd hardly noticed the gushing water stop.

"Somebody had elaborate booty chaos." Hank stood poking his head in the door, turning as Garth ran up. "You're supposed to wait till *after* gobbling the gobbler to nuke the bathroom, son."

Tony shied away, squirming his little head around behind mine. He'd grown since I last saw him. Hardly fitting in my arms anymore, he wrapped around my shoulders like a furry boa.

"Not me, Mr. Hank," Garth said in his defense. Late to the party — likely from turning off the water main — he was still festooned in green garland from redecorating the bar. Out with the Samhain, in with the Yule. Much as I wasn't a fan.

With the newly wrecked bathroom, I was suddenly very glad we were closed for Turkey Day, though we still had a few wayward souls among us.

"You've caused a big mess, Tony," I scratched his furry belly. He poked his head around to my face.

I felt his contrition in the way he moved, the way he held his beak slightly open, and eyes downcast as if he wanted to say *I'm sorry.*

"It's okay, I forgive you," I reassured him, stroking the mane coming in around his face. Growing up so fast. "But you need to clean this up, young man."

Tony trilled, jumping from my arms to splash along the tile — stubby legs scooting him along to the bits of broken porcelain. He began nomming away at his disaster area.

"Mistress," a dripping Evette came to my elbow, "what exactly is...um...Tony?" She watched the rokuichi at work — beak crunching shattered toilet bowl bites like cereal, tossing the rubble down his gullet. He scurried under the broken door to get at bits of the other toilet.

"Good question," Hank raised a fuzzy eyebrow. "Hungry little critter, in'n he."

"My friend," I said simply. I already had a headache and really didn't feel like explaining the rokuichi and my twisted tunnel adventures, so I left it at that.

"Yes, Mistress Molly," Evette replied quickly, eyes downcast. Maybe I'd put a little sternness in my voice.

"Yes, Mistress Molly," Maya mocked from the hallway, curlers in her black hair, red silken robe clinging to exaggerated curves. She yawned. "What's the fuss?"

"Evette," I ignored Maya, "I've asked you to just call me Molly, please."

"But Mistress Molly is just so much more fun." Maya smiled, red robe tightening to shiny latex, hair slicked back severely. "Don't worry, Evette," she turned, crop in hand, "I can be your mistress." Maya batted smoky eyes at my bartender, who gulped. Maya's mercurial form always astonished me, changing at a whim, quick as thought. I'd learned quite a lot from her, but I wasn't *that* good. And I certainly wasn't in the mood.

"Oh, don't start, Maya," I complained. "It's too early." I hadn't even had my coffee yet, and people were being far too jolly.

"Yeth, Mithtress," she muffled around the gag suddenly in her mouth, hands tied before her.

The cutest little rock grinder noises chortled in the bathroom.

"Ooooh, no," Maya schitzed, appearing beside the two gawkers in the doorway. "No, no, no. Not *them*. I thought I got away from 'em when I left the flatiron." Hands thrown in exasperation, she stomped off in her typical dramatic fashion.

I sighed. I still wasn't quite sure how to deal with Maya. She was my friend, but she'd shown up looking for Felix. No response from him, be-tee-dubs — I couldn't help checking my phone. You'd think the longer it was, the less I'd check. Nope.

She wasn't what I'd thought at first. It was all part of her cabaret act. She'd gotten lonely without Felix's booty calls and our girl talks, so she took her show on the road, now setting up in the Last Chance — eight shows a week, two being midnight reviews on Friday and Saturday. She was a bonafide hit.

And in just two weeks, to boot! Maya had shown up at the Last Chance wearing nothing but a bow gathering up red ribbon tied...strategically.

"Felix, love, where are you?" She burst on the scene. "I'm all wrapped up and ready for your tree," she called, passing a Garth stricken dumb. Used to not being noticed, Maya thought nothing of it and strutted straight past and into the stunned bar. "Feeelix," she swayed among the tables, looking for her desired tryst. The ribbon tugged at her curves, squeezing as she bent to and fro.

"Maya!" I'd called to her, a shade shy of scandalized. "Come. Here." I sent my shadow around her, draping across her pale flesh, tingling — the touch electric.

"Oh!" Maya gasped at the shadow. "Molly!" She squeed and clippitied over to the bar in some seriously high heels, bouncing along the way. "Mwah, mwah," she fake-kissed each cheek. "Where's our boy?"

"Maya, hon," I gestured around. "Maybe magic some clothes? People are staring." The whole crowd. Every single jaw on the floor. Maya was not subtle.

"But this feels so luxurious," Maya stroked my shadow, sending shivers up my spine. "Besides," she laughed, "only you can..." she trailed off, seeing the eyes on her, "...see me?"

She blinked, eyes widening in shock.

"They can see me?" She jumped up and down, draped shadow dropping, ribbon falling loose. "They can see me!" Tears formed in her eyes. "They can *see* me." The weight of loneliness melted from her shoulders as she wept. "They can see me!" she shrilled. Startled by the revelation of her visible nakedness, she blushed and vanished, reappearing behind me in a terry cloth robe clutched tight at the neck. "Why can they see me?" Suspicious.

The bar erupted in laughter.

I couldn't help but giggle. Maya's antics never ceased to amaze, but rarely did her shyness show.

"I don't think they've seen anyone quite like you, hon." I smiled reassuringly at her, temerity taking hold of her mood.

"Am I out?" Hope cracked Maya's voice. "Is it over?"

My heart broke a little. Brash, bold, ever confident, Maya never showed this kind of vulnerability — except when it came to escaping the twist. I hugged her.

"I don't know," I told her honest. "But you're here, so maybe you are?"

"Where's *here* anyway?" Maya took a good look around for the first time since she'd made her grand entrance. "And where's Felix? He just told me to meet him wherever this dot is." She held up a phone. Felix's? "Can you read it?"

She couldn't read. My heart sank. She was still twisted. I swallowed, gathering my thoughts before I answered. Had Felix really planned to meet her here, or was he up to something?

"This," I swept my hand over the bar, "is the Last Chance. I own the place," I admitted, adding a mumbled, "apparently."

"Nice digs! Moving up in the world," Maya beamed. "How'd that happen?"

"Won a bet," I said, tempted to snark *'or lost'* on the end of it. I was still deciding. "Felix set me up," I did add.

"Well that was thoughtful. So where is our patron saint?" Maya's eyes twinkled at me.

Mine, I averted.

"I don't know." He'd blatantly handed back my main tracker, and the phone — yes, I was tracking his phone — wasn't pinging. "Can I see that?" If he'd given it to Maya, that might explain it.

"Sure, toots," Maya handed it over. Not Felix's, just one like it. "You can have it. I don't like those things." Her mouth made a distasteful turn, pulling the robe tighter. "I need to sit down," she said, suddenly looking exhausted. Poor thing, I had no idea what it took for her to get this far.

"You can sit on my lap if you want, little girl," a surly mall Santa chuckled a tad ruefully. Crushed velvet suit — emphasis on crushed, along with caked and crumpled — sat at the bar swilling Weihenstephaner. The suit ill fit, being made for a jolly fatter man than he. "Ho, ho, ho," he coughed, no twinkle in his eye. Merely contempt.

"Naughty Santa," Maya chided half-heartedly, "who you callin' a ho?" She stuck her hand on her hip in a pose that said *Mhmm, I didn't think so*, stopping just short of snapping.

Weeks later, he was still at the bar. Cheeks rosy from the booze. He'd made his way down under, now swilling Foster's — prefer a VB myself, for Australian beer.

"Shouldn't you be in a parade or something?" I waved vaguely in the direction of a TV showing *the* parade. Like there's only the one. For many, it was the beginning of Christmas spirit. Seeing the singing tree, watching Santa in his sleigh. For me, it turned my stomach — decorating with the corpses of my kin.

"You see," he leaned, "that's exactly the problem right there." Santa spun on the TV showing Macy's. "They expect me to be everywhere! All at once!" Santa was toasty. "I'm spread too thin," he sulked. "No respect for the proper order of seasons, no no no." He looked at me over grimy round glasses perched atop a ruddy nose. "For goodness's sake, the jackals are even celebrating Christmas in *July*!"

He toppled from his stool in tipsy aggravation.

"On that, Santa, we can agree." I sent my shadow to set him aright — handy thing it was becoming. I guess even a fake St Nick could lose his way and wind up here. "For what it's worth, I prefer Halloween myself. Find Christmas' attempt to take over the calendar atrocious."

"Oh, don't blame that on Christmas, little girl. No, no, no," He shook his scraggly beard at me. "That's *all* greed's doing." For a moment, he looked entirely downtrodden. His shoulders slumped, all trace of merriment replaced by regret. "We just can't compete," St Nick said a bit sullenly, retreating into his beer again.

"Well, just wanted you to know the gents is out of order, so you'll have to wait til the ladies' is empty." Did this guy think he *was* Santa?

"No problem there," the mall Santa said, "I can hold it for a long sleigh ride. One time..." he trailed off, eyes locked on the door through which a giant among moose strode.

"Elder!" I hopped the bar, shadow barely keeping up, as I ran for my friend. "You should have told me you were coming," I chattered, "I may have some pumpk..."

I screamed, seeing blood on his should-be silvered forelocks. I'd been so excited, I hadn't noticed he was hurt.

Elder stumbled forward, one eye swollen shut, the other wild. I barely caught him with my shadow, the weight crushing me as he dripped blood all over. Distantly, I heard feet behind me.

"GARTH!" I called to one of the feet, having come at my scream. The giant of a bouncer got under the wounded moose, helping me carry Elder to a booth.

"Geez-o-Pete," Hank said, hobbling up beside me. He assessed the wound with a seemingly practiced eye. "Evette, sweetie, get my case."

Can't Blame the Moose

I CAN ONLY DESCRIBE what happened next as a miracle. Bless you, Hank.

That's all I'm allowed to say, anyway. Golden light and a sweet song later, Elder was good as new. Not that he'd actually been all that hurt, the drama queen.

"I don't care if most of it *wasn't* your blood," I swatted Elder's shoulder after panic mode ended. "And that you were just tired. I was still super scared." I hugged up against him.

I understood what Elder said just fine, but I'd gotten used to the fact that no one else around me did. And so they all looked at me like a crazy person as I narrated for the both of us. Only, politely, since I *was* the boss and all.

"So, whose blood was it?" Maya had entered the chat. Hysterics passed, she sat on the bar next to Elder, draping one shapely leg off the edge.

"Wolf's blood," I said. Elder sat on his haunches by the bar now that his dire peril was over. Garth kindly popped the top on a keg for him. Even sitting, he was still a good eight feet tall. "Lots of wolves," I side-eyed Elder.

"Must be hungry or stupid," Hank observed. "My vote's stupid," he toasted the stately moose. Elder bowed his head in thanks, careful not to take anyone out with his antlers.

"Either way, he got jumped..." I started, but Elder shook his head. "No?"

I can tell what he's saying, but the translation isn't always perfect. He ran through it again, slowly this time, taking a long draught of beer afterward.

"Okay, sorry," I started again, the crowd eagerly awaiting the tale. "A pack of parachute wolves jumped out of the sky, courtesy of the Canadian Air Force."

"Stupid geese," Hank interjected.

"And started stabbing at him with knives." That part hardly seemed believable. "Are you sure about that?"

Elder snorted a yes.

"Okay, okay," I wasn't going to fight it. "They had knives. What I don't get is why Canadians were dropping armed para-wolves on you."

"Seems totally impolite," Maya stroked Elder behind the ear. "Just minding your own business when, WHAM," she clapped her hands together, "get hit with a wolf."

"Well, all that matters is you're safe now." I put my arm around Elder's neck. "How'd you know I was here, anyway?"

Elder turned his head away. Ashamed? If he were human, he'd be studying his shoelaces intently at that moment. Maybe even whistling. That was the vibe I got.

"Elder?"

Now he kicked at the dirt and shrugged, still not looking me in the eye. So I climbed up on the bar and took his face in my hands. Sometimes you just have to be direct.

"You weren't looking for me." I peered into his deep eyes, seeing what had taken place. The pain. The fear. He wasn't coming to me for comfort. "Why were you looking for Felix? What could he have done?"

"Can't blame the moose, Missy," Hank said. "Memory or not, Felix is..." He hesitated. "Well, something else."

"What?" I knew that instinctively — it's why I followed him around — but I got the feeling Hank *knew*. He'd experienced a version of Felix I'd never seen. Close and seemingly too personal.

"That's his tea to spill," Hank sipped some Crown. I took the drink from his lips. Hank sputtered. Evette gasped.

"Out with it." I was tired of being in the dark. It was lonely — only a lantern keeping the night at bay.

"My lips are sealed, Missy." Hank sat cross-armed and stared at me. The doddering old man he presented himself as was a lie. A front. A ruse — cleverness debatable. The old devil still had steel in him. But I couldn't back down.

"Hmph!" I tipped his Crown back and slammed it on the bar.

"Tell you what, Missy." Hank squinted one eye at me as he fished around in his pocket. "I'll tell if you win." The coin he showed gleamed gold and was engraved with a skull laughing on one side, screaming on the reverse.

"And if I lose?" Elder shook his head, advising me not to wager.

"Why, nothing much." Hank smiled his devilish smile, a gleam lit in his eyes.

I was in hell. I'd lost count of how many times I'd lost WHAMagedon by the third day. Non-stop Christmas cheer for two weeks and counting. Over the house speakers. On the TVs I was tempted to break. Everywhere I looked, too much merry.

"Never trusting that old devil again," I muttered as the bells on my shoes jingled and jangled. Furious. "How the hell do you win a coin flip and still lose?"

"What a fascinating proposition!" An older guy, hair as white as mine, had approached the bar unnoticed while I'd been going slightly mad. "How does someone accomplish that feat?" We were technically open, but the crowds hadn't yet arrived to blissfully drown out the nauseating cheer.

"Pick tails on a coin that literally reads 'tails you lose.'" My face soured at the memory. Cheater.

"R. T. F. And C. Always," the stranger nodded, a diamond glinting in the dim light — a single stud in his ear. "Read the F-ing Coin," he amended at my blank stare, laughing at his own joke. "They'll bite you every time. Speaking of bite, got any Rye?"

"Sure do." I pulled an Old Forester bottle from beneath the counter, supposedly. Had to keep stock where it couldn't be St Nicked. Thankfully he was napping some off at the end of the bar next to Elder.

"Bless you, I mean truly." He eyed the bottle gratefully. "And make it a double," he said, laying a velvet bag on the bar. As he did, I noticed a ring on his pinky — gold, studded with three diamonds. The man liked his bling.

I poured out a healthy dram for the white-haired gent.

"Oh ho, heavy-handed!" His eyes widened in delight, then he looked around. "Does the owner know you're that generous?" He said it kinda sly as he took the double.

"Of course," I smiled, fluttering my eyelashes. I didn't care to elaborate. Instead, I poured one for myself and toasted. "Cheers."

"Cheers to that," he laughed, drinking the toast. I finished it. Rye wasn't my favorite, but the proof was there. "Whoaho, young lady!"

I didn't have anything on Felix or Sassy, but I *could* keep pace with a two-thousand-pound moose. Usually. After his run-in with the para-wolves, he'd been hitting the bottle a little hard, drinking himself under the table. Well — on the table in this case. His antlers hadn't escaped Hank's rampant festooning — strung with blasphemous garland as he slept.

"Care to keep up?" Returning my attention to my customer, I waggled my eyebrows and teased him with the bottle. Might as well make this hell interesting.

In response, he cocked his head with a crooked smile and opened the velvet bag, spilling diamonds across the bar. The clear ice sparkled on the ebon wood like stars in the cold winter sky.

He talked as I poured. A lot. He'd just been to Vegas — lucky bastard — and a few other places hunting for the strangest things. Along the way, he dropped some names that were supposed to impress me, but didn't. Damn, did he like the sound of his own voice. We were on the third round of rye when he finally hit on me.

"You look quite festive." He nodded to my ugly Christmas sweater and assorted paraphernalia thus far unremarked upon. Somehow neglected in his verbacious ramble.

"Lost a bet," I tossed back another, "remember?"

"Ah, the coin." Realization dawned in his eyes. "RTFC," he reiterated over his still-full glass. He seemed ready to launch into another oral regalia when Elder started snoring at the end of the bar, startling my new drinking buddy — and waking the mall Santa — when he twitched his rack.

"You're falling behind," I nodded, pouring myself another.

"Did that moose snore?" He seemed entirely perplexed by the proposition.

"Does that when he drinks too much," I said, pulling ahead in the count.

"Amazing." He finally knocked his rye back. "I thought it was a trophy head!"

"So, how did you wind up here, friend?" He didn't seem *lost*; in fact, he seemed to know right where he was — like he'd been here before.

"I heard it was under new management." He looked around the bar as people started to trickle in. "Much friendlier," he added, looking my way. Not quite predatory, but still presumptive in an obnoxious way.

"Thanks, we try." Still not elaborating. I wasn't sure which new management he was talking about.

"Where is the dear boy?" He asked this over his fourth rye, eyebrows raised.

"Who?" I had an idea. The one we all wondered about.

"The new owner! Felix — he called himself last we met. I heard he sent that asshole Hector packing," he laughed. "And good riddance!" Anger flashed briefly across his affable face. Guess Hector wasn't all that popular.

Felix apparently was, though. Every new face walking through that door seemed to be looking for him. I'd like to know where the blue blazes he was myself.

"Felix isn't here," I said carefully. I didn't know who this guy was, but he seemed to know Felix. "And he doesn't own the Last Chance." I stiffened my back, jingle bells ringing as I stamped my heel in slight offense. My shadow rippled in displeasure.

"Oh!" His eyes widened, watching my shadow with a knowing eye. "My apologies, young lady." He slid another diamond toward me. My shadow took it. "I meant no offense," he held his hand across his heart, "truly."

"See you put all that stocking coal I left you to good use," Santa hiccuped as he wobbled his way up to us, butting in.

"All five hundred years worth!" Felix's friend laughed as he hefted the velvet pouch with a flourish.

Santa ignored the odd comment. Instead, his bleary eyes met mine. "S'the loo fixed?" One eye blinked, then the other, as he asked.

"Sure is," I hooked my thumb over my shoulder. "Thanks for holding it!" Mall Santa waved as he wobbled on. "Apology accepted." I returned my attention to the rock. "Is it real?"

"Of course!" His own back stiffened, head raising like a prairie dog. "No true alchemist walks around with fakes."

And it clicked. Vegas trip. Diamond in his ear. Felix hadn't said anything about alchemy, but that made an odd amount of sense. He wasn't wearing all black, but...

"You must be St Germain." Felix had said he talked a lot.

"Indeed! The Comte de St Germain, Marquis de Montserrat, and various other titles as have been bestowed upon me, at your service," the Count said, thickly French, bowing slightly.

"Glad to meet you, your Countyness," I laughed, faking a curtsy. Those are just awkward in pants.

"I'm glad you met me, too," he ebulled. "I've never met myself. Must be a wonderful experience," St Germain said almost to himself. "How lucky you are to meet me for the first time!" He leaned forward to clink my glass.

"Don't believe a word that loudmouth says, Missy." Hank came in, followed by Garth toting a suspicious box. The old devil hopped up beside St Germain and laughed, a smile in his eyes. "Took you long enough."

"There's the liar." The Count turned to hug Hank. "You told me Felix got rid of Hector, and here this lovely young lady stands in his stead. What gives?"

"He did." Unhelpful as always, Hank just let people carry on. I rather admired that, except when it was turned on me. Stupid coin. "She's alright," Hank said for the thousandth time. I guess I was alright.

"Garth," St Germain nodded to the silent giant when he realized Hank wasn't going to elaborate.

"Count," Garth nodded back. "Mr. Hank, where you want this?"

"Over on the stage." I felt my stomach drop.

"What is it?" St Germain craned his neck, trying to peek.

"Take a look," Hank waved. A wicked glint filled his eyes as they met mine. Oh no.

St Germain stood and pulled down a box flap. His eyebrow rose.

"Karaoke!?" Pure excitement filled his face.

"Christmas Karaoke," Hank hooted, slapping his knee. "Twelve days of it!"

Okay, *now* I was in hell.

Where Are You, Felix Chance?

BREATH FOGGED THE AIR as I thought. The chill felt good in my nostrils. It smelt like snow. Briefly, I wondered if it actually snowed wherever here was. Of course it would, it snowed everywhere — eventually. And much was called for — there had been many berries, and the wooly bear I'd seen had been quite dark. Signs are everywhere, if you know.

Even without the muffle of snow, the delicious hush of night bled the pressure from my ears — constant revelry can really get to you.

I'd made it through eight days of Christmas so far — we were up to the maids-a-milking and Maya was having a field day with the uniforms — but I wasn't sure I could make it to the twelve drummers drumming.

Out of habit, I checked my phone. I could read it, thankfully, but no new messages. No activity on Felix's end.

"Care for a smoke?" St Germain stepped out of the joyous caroling-karaoke and into the cold. I thought I caught a snippet of Mariah. When I left, Elder had been bugling to 'Frosty the Snowman.' I loved that moose, but he couldn't carry a tune.

"No thanks," I exhaled a plume at him, "I can make my own."

"So you can, dear girl." He took out a cigarette case, monogrammed with StG, naturally. The metal was unlike anything I'd ever seen. It gleamed grey-green. Not shiny like silver or gold, not dull like gunmetal. "I can see why the dear boy likes you." I doubted he meant my clever wit as he took out a cigarette. The case was seamless, unfolding like cloth.

"Who said Felix likes me?" I laughed. "I just tag along. Probably finds me annoying." Felix had put up with me for a while now, but I hadn't really given him a choice. When I did, he left me behind. Even when I didn't. I checked my phone — rude, I know, so sue me — to find nothing.

St Germain considered me a moment, eyes old yet clear. Deep and cold, like the underside of an iceberg. He struck a metal rod from the cigarette case, lighting his smoke with an indigo flame. "Naphtha," he said as I perplexed, extinguishing the rod as it slid into the case.

I tilted my head, unfamiliar with the word.

"Neither flammable nor inflammable." Indigo flame lit the dark again with a strike. This time he shook the rod. The flame upon it danced but did not go out. It smelled like kerosene. "Great stuff," the purported alchemist said. "Came upon it quite by accident centuries back as I distilled a mixture of..." He stopped mid-sentence and waved his hand. "Matters not. Won't ignite unless you strike it, won't go out unless you quash it." He slid the fire home again, snuffing the flame. "Even in water."

His explanation confused me even more.

"If the boy didn't like you," he returned from his side track, "you would not be *here*." St Germain gestured back to the Last Chance. "Where time spent is not reckoned against the seconds of one's life."

That's a sentence that needs unpacking.

"How long have you known Felix?" Judging by the catch in my throat, I felt a change in subject appropriate. It was getting colder.

"*Felix?*" St Germain quirked an eyebrow, silver smoke rising from the tip of his cigarette. "Not long at all, I'm afraid," he flicked ash, lips turned bitter.

"But he said in Vegas you knew him," I recalled.

"*Knew*," the alchemist pointed with his cigarette between his fingers. "Past tense is quite appropriate." He took a drag, staring up into the night sky. "Before that," he shrugged, "centuries." St Germain sounded wistful.

I laughed. Felix had told me some whoppers — and backed most of them up, truth be told — but he'd never claimed to be an immortal himself like the fellow before me.

"How long have you been wandering about?" It was St Germain's turn to change the subject. "Do your kin call it Rhumshpringa as well?"

No. They didn't. Defenses up. How much did this stranger know?

I don't know what kind of face I made at that, but it must have been unkindly because the Count stubbed out his smoke, no longer pursuing the topic.

"Let's get you inside," he said instead. "You're looking cold, and I feel a rousing round of song coming on!" He laughed as he held his arm out to escort me back inside. Decorations aside, I did like being inside in the dark Yuletide. "How about 'Holly Jolly Christmas'?"

I stiffened briefly as he winked. Then carried on, barely breaking stride as we reached the door. He knew. Before I could begin to suss out how much, out in the trees, there arose such a clatter. I sprang from the stoop to see what was the matter.

The dim grey gave no hints as to what crashed through the woods. Crumble and crack, the boughs gave way to scarlet and lavender, albeit begrudgingly, as the branches tugged tufts of the fine fabrics among the snags — some grips stronger than others, alive with intent.

"Please, safe passage for one of the People." Hazel eyes pleaded with mine from a young face, young as my own.

"The who?" There were all kinds of people in the world, but I wasn't terribly familiar with any who capitalized it. "Nevermind," I waved the line of thinking away. Questions later. She was panicking. "You have safe passage, all are welcome at the Last Chance."

She stumbled, toe catching in the dirt. St Germain caught the woman as she began to tumble. Spry belying his age, he'd moved before even my shadow.

"Enchante," he carefully helped her steady. She tensed.

"Down boy," I laughed at the hopeless flirt, taking the newcomer by the hand. "He can't help it."

"It is by second nature." St Germain dipped his head and raised his hands. "I mean no ill."

"Come inside and get warm."

Inside, the lights were low and the spots were hot as Maya and the mall Santa did a rousing rendition of "Santa Baby" as only they could. I took silk-scarves by the hand and led her across the back of the crowded room. She seemed to cringe as we walked, pulling her shawl tighter and closing in on herself.

I began to make a joke about not liking karaoke either, when I noticed her eyes darting wildly over the crowd — reflections of other places flashed in their depths. Her lips worked wordlessly, forming the words 'so many people.'

"Get Evette to make some hot tea and bring it to my office," I conscripted St Germain.

As we entered my office, Tony was munching on tinsel. He was a kind soul. Hank snuck in every night to festoon — I imagine Evette helped, Hank not being terribly spry — and every day, Tony nommed it away.

"Hello baby," I scratched his furry white head, "thanks for having my back." He relished in the pets. "Don't worry, he's nice....Miss...Peoples? Was it?" I knew it wasn't, but I couldn't very well keep calling her silk-scarves. I'm not Felix.

"Deirdre," she corrected, slipping the silk scarf off her head, shaking out untamed curls. "Where am I?" She looked around my tiny office. Browned all over. Fake wood paneling straight from the eighties. Smoke-stained drop tile. Bronze lamps and a crumpled-in couch — also brown. Though I suspect it may have once been yellow or even blue.

"My bar," I said, finally owning it, "it's the Last Chance."

"Last chance for what?" Deirdre's willowy eyes met mine, seeking answers. I shrugged, breaking contact.

"Who knows?" I said it honestly. I didn't have a clue. Neither did Hank — and I'd asked him straight. Terrible poker face. He can *not tell* me all the things he wants, but he just can't lie. "I think it's different for everyone."

"Makes a sort of metaphysical sense." She tucked her legs under her on the couch. "Honestly, I've never had this happen." Her lips pursed.

"What? Wound up in a dive bar?"

"No," she serened. "Not ended up where I was going."

"Oh." Now I was confused. "Did your car break down? It's dangerous walking dark forest at night," I said. "Especially in this cold."

"I don't, like, drive," she smiled. "I walk. I walk wherever I want to go, and end up there a few minutes later. Super easy." Deirdre bit her lip. "Except tonight, I found myself in an unkind wood. My way mislaid."

"Hate when that happens," I agreed out of habit. "But the woods aren't unkind, just misunderstood."

"Too many eyes," she shuddered. "They totally glowed. Stalking me."

I laughed. Couldn't help myself.

"Oh, they're just curious, letting you know they're there." I smiled to reassure her. "They're saying, 'I am alive and I have mucosal membranes.'"

Why did I say that? That was an odd thing to say. Deirdre looked at me, stuck for a reply. We were saved from awkward by a knock at the door.

"Your tea, Mistress," Evette called from the other side. Yay, more, different awkward. I briefly wondered if I ordered her not to call me 'Mistress,' she would obey or just say 'Yes, Mistress,' and keep on doing it. I sighed.

"Thank you, Evette." I didn't chide or protest; I simply tried to ignore it as I poured tea for my guest. The fragrance of rose hips filled the small room. Deirdre seemed to relax the moment I handed her the cup, melting down into the couch.

"This smells so delicious," she said, taking a sip. "And is."

Another knock at the door. Seriously?

"Missy," Hank broke in, "you better get out here," he said before he saw my guest. "Op, sorry. You're busy." He made to pull the door to as I stopped him.

"What's wrong?" I couldn't catch a break with this lot. Much preferred dashing when trouble came in.

"Well, ah," Hank hedged, "there're some gnomes come in and your mall Santa's getting rowdy with 'em."

I shot Deirdre a pained look of apology mingled with *Enjoy the tea I can't before it gets cold* and *BRB.* She smiled and nodded, inhaling the calming herbal.

Out in the bar, three gnomes stood on top of one another, the top-most in Santa's face.

"Look buster," he jabbed knife hands, "we don't work for you! Quit tryin' ta order us around!" I guessed they were gnomes anyway. White beards, red hats, straight out of a garden.

The bottom gnome kicked at Santa's shins for emphasis. Mall Santa, his cheeks extra rosy, didn't take kindly to that, winding up. Swing and a miss as the top gnome leapt over the drunken haymaker to yank Santa's hat down around his ears.

"Why you little..." He spun. I giggled. Sorry. I couldn't help it. It was too ridiculous.

"Alright, that's enough," I broke in, clapping my hands. Garth grabbed a gnome in each hand. My shadow held the other as I helped Santa up. "What the heck has gotten into you lot?"

"He started it!" The middle gnome pointed vigorously at Santa, wriggling in Garth's grip. "We came in for a pint after work and he gets all up in our face."

"You ungrateful little elves," Santa fumed. "After all the centuries of gainful employment..."

"Wohoah, Santa!" St Germain came to the fray, Maya at his side. "They're not elves, man. Take another look. They're fjøsnisser!" Giddy is how I'd describe his face at that moment.

"Finally! An educated and traveled gentleman." The top gnome turned toward St Germain. "Thank you!"

"But," Santa looked confused, squinting at the gnomes he thought were elves, "but who'll make the toys?"

Maya slinked her hand around drunk Santa. "C'mon, Santa baby," she drew him away.

"The children will be so disappointed," he rambled. "The reindeer quit," his drunken stupor continued, "joke's on them, though," he laughed, "gotta wear those stupid safety antlers now. They look ridiculous! Ungrateful little..."

"Of course they do," Maya consoled. I shot her a grateful look.

"Gentlemen," I turned to the gnomes, "my apologies for that. Next round's on the house, but please try to keep the tempers in check?"

They each doffed their caps and swept a bow. I poured each a pint as they climbed up to the stools.

"Sorry 'bout that," the top gnome said. "Bit twitchy after midwinter. Come off the longest night shift and all."

"What do fjøsnisser — did I say that right? — what do you do?" I was a bit intrigued. I'd never met a gnome before, not that I'd known.

"We're hunters," the middle provided. "Keep the baddies at bay."

"Winter solstice is *the* worst!" Bottom upped his pint, draining it. "Everything bumps that night."

"You don't say." St Germain sat at the bar. That was my cue to exit as the gnomes turned their attention to him. Not that I didn't like the alchemist, but he just talked *soooo* much and seemed to know even more.

I still had to figure out how much St Germain knew about me and my kind. First, though, tea. If there were any left.

I stepped back slowly, trying not to draw attention to my absence, as Evette appeared to pour more rounds.

Inconspicuous has never been my strong suit, seeing as I bumped into Elder rounding the bar. He swayed and hiccuped pleasantly — I'd soaked some pumpkins with vodka for him. It's why he loves me best. And why he'd forgive me for nearly knocking him over.

"Oh Elder, I'm sorry, I wasn't paying attention. A kiss?" I looked up to see a sprig of mistletoe in his rack. It wasn't really a moose I wanted to kiss under it, but why not?

I gave him a smooch and he finished the job I'd started, collapsing to the floor to snore it off. I patted him goodnight and was off to ask my guest some questions.

Answers awaited my return, though I'd not yet asked — Deirdre had drawn the tarot in my absence.

It was an unfamiliar layout, though it looked suspiciously like a tree. I squinted.

"Evergreen spread," Deirdre said, handing me a steaming cuppa. "I asked Evette for another pot. I hope you don't mind," answering my questions as they formed.

I took the teacup gladly, inhaling the steam as I considered the cards. I knew them all, but not their meaning in this spread. At a glance six, Queen, King of coins. Charity, blessed good sense, success and security — all good. Two cups, shared by a balanced pair. Lovely. Three and ten of swords, heartbreak and suffering followed by inescapable disaster — don't like that. Not at all. The Moon hiding her secrets — how appropriate.

"You know the tarot." Not a question. Deirdre's hazel eyes flashed emeralds at me briefly.

"A bit," I smiled, "but not this spread."

"I love this spread for the end of a year," she bubbled, "super popular on my channel, too." She took a sip and went on, pointing to the positions. "Pine wreath to complete," for the six, "purged before years end." On to the ten. "Log of Yule shows themes for the new year," she had the decency to grimace at the apparent doom. "Mistletoe shows what we can grow," sliding to the Queen. "You seem familiar," she said, looking to my side, "ah, so here you are," she smiled. "Focus on you, boo."

I fidgeted a bit, quieting my thoughts lest she hear them. Because apparently...she smiled and continued. I stopped thinking.

"The Yule tree shows our gifts, the talents we may draw on." Her finger landed on the cups. My lacking pair. "And the candle it holds to shine the way," fingers slid to the King suited, of course. "Holly for protection," she said as I bristled, "the how and the what." Her hand covered the elusive moon, keeping secrets. Kept safe.

Too close. Too close to home. First St Germain, now her?

"Lastly, the Ivy that binds all to peace." Her hand waved to heartbreak and sorrow, three swords stabbing a rose. "Remember, there are two sides to every card, boo. It's not always all bad." She flipped the card in question, turning pain into healing. "It's how we choose."

"So," I sorted my thoughts. There are many ways to read the cards. "What's your take on it then? Which should I flip?"

"NGL, it's going to be rough," she pointed to the ten, "but you've got this," over to the Queen. "Strength will come from the heartbreak," she flipped the three back, "just not the one you think."

"If I'm the Queen, who's the King lighting the way?" And where were we on the timeline, I didn't ask. Spreads like this aren't all yet-to-pass, most are markers fixed.

"Where's Felix?" The sudden turn threw me. Her eyes narrowed on mine.

"You know Felix?" Stupid question. *Of course* she knew Felix. Everyone seemed to.

"Grandma keeps asking me to deliver messages," as if that explained everything, "but I totally can't find him and wound up here." A crack of bitterness through her serenity. "Super weird."

"That's been happening a lot," I grumbled. "People keep showing up asking, and I'd damn well like to know myself."

"You don't need him, you know." Another twist, focused back on me. "He gave you what you need to shine." She pointed to the candle King. "To be safe."

Goddammit, there's that word again.

"I don't want to be safe!" I stormed out of the office, mind reeling. I didn't want to be safe. I wanted to be with Felix.

Out in the bar, I jumped up on stage, bumping poor Garth from the mic. Boos flew at me from the darkness as I glared through the spotlight.

"Alright everyone shut up a second!" My eyes adjusted enough I could see the outline of the crowd. "Show of hands, who here's looking for Felix?"

The crowd quieted. Slowly, one hand raised.

Then another.

And another. Until the whole crowd had their hand in the air.

"Where are you, Felix Chance?"

Jamais Vu

I FOUND MYSELF LOST in a stolen day — living my life a second go-round, one piece at a time. And there, I was stuck.

Surprise.

Hers was a bright soul, shining and new, and her daddy didn't like me. Anyone really. No one was good enough for his baby — not me, not the butcher's boy, not the noble drawn from afar. None of us. But I'll get to that in a minute. Lot to catch up on.

I didn't remember being born, though I must have been, and I didn't remember dying, at least not yet. I get the feeling it didn't much agree with me — cause it never seemed to stick.

That one was an eye-opener.

There she was, my Dena, long hair falling down her back as she rose from the bed — our bed — gripping the blanket around her against the chill. Though I imagine it was more to catch sight of me uncovered — or at least my ego likes to believe that.

"Thief," I teased her, grabbing the blanket, and pulling her back to the bed with a giggle.

"Stooop," she swatted me as I kissed her. "Nature calls."

"It does indeed," I growled, kissing her again.

"Just a minute, husband." She slipped from my arms and made her way to the privy. *Husband.* The thought still made me giddy.

Her 'minute' had long gone. Though I'd lived it again a thousand times now — never growing tired of it, of her — it always had the sweet taste of that first kiss.

The room faded around me, replaced by a river of stars in the night sky wheeling above. Breathtaking grandeur, taken in with the woman I loved. Pure heaven.

"Do you ever think about how strange it is we met? The chance of it all?" Dena turned to me in the darkness, shadow against the starlight. I had to laugh inside — strange chance, indeed.

"What brought that thought on?" Not in on the joke yet, my old self found it less amusing.

"Just this." She swept her arm across the speckled sky. "Of all the possibilities that led us to this moment in this time." Dena had always been a deep thinker, even when such was not common — but she never was common. Genuine awe and gratitude suffused her voice. The world was a miracle through her eyes — benefit of a shiny new soul, I suppose — and I loved every second of it.

"I'm simply grateful," I said. Even by then, I'd seen a thing or two. Learned a few too many lessons. Forgot some things, remembered others I shouldn't. A bit weary of it already, I felt, though only by the vaguest of feelings.

She'd made me happy and hopeful then, as she had from the moment I'd laid eyes on her.

Painting along the riverbank in some forgotten town, that's where I'd found her. Alone, and the cause of much spectacle because of it.

Well, once people noticed her. At the time, I had no idea how anyone could *not* notice her — after all, I had only eyes for her, and a mere handful of tricks to my old name — but there she was, sitting at her easel among the comings and goings of dozens who paid her no mind at all. Until I saw her.

So deep was her concentration upon the rippling river that she'd nary noticed my approach — so I thought. I kept a respectful distance, gazing at the very same river, racking my brain for clever words.

And then, awe struck me dumb as my eyes stared at the river within her painting — *also* rippling. Not by virtue of verisimilitude or capitulating to the over-the-top stylization growing in popularity at the time. It simply *moved* as if imbued by animate life.

Not only that, but the very leaves she painted upon the riverbank trees began to rustle in an unfelt breeze.

"Remarkable," I breathed, barely above a whisper. So transfixed, I hardly noticed her shock at the single utterance, nor the kerfuffle her sudden appearance had caused.

None had seen her until I had, and then they all did.

At first, people were startled to see a painter where none had been before. And then, they realized the painter wearing pants was a woman and became scandalized. Said pants, brown in color, tucked into boots while she sported a tasteful maroon vest and a large hat to shade her eyes. Entirely amiss with the right proper ladies' dresses with the foppy skirts and lace décolletage, she was guilty of one simple crime. Being a woman.

And for that they tried to burn her. Because, duh, witch. Appearing from nowhere? Wearing pants? Guilty, open and shut. Such uncivil times. I'm glad we outgrew that.

The burning part, anyway. Need to work on the rest.

"How do we get her out?" This I
asked of my closest confidant, the still-blonde, not-yet-immortal-merely-long-lived alchemist St Germain, also then known by another name. He'd only just begun his

crafting of the clock I'd asked of him. Tinkering with time, really. The rest would come much, much later. When time was on our side.

We sat plotting in a dimly lit pub, tucked away in a corner designed for such circumspection. Rather, I sat plotting; he sat drinking.

"Why would you want to spring a witch?" He mugged his ale. "She put a spell on you already?" A sly wink followed.

"She's not a witch," I protested, a bit too loud. *She's my wife,* I added to finish the quote to myself. "It was my fault she was seen," my lips said instead. And it was. She had been perfectly fine until I noticed her sitting there, acknowledging her presence when none had. I hadn't yet learned how rude it was to *see* people who did not want to be *seen.*

"Fair, fair," he relented. "But if she can paint unmolested — while wearing trousers no less! — surely she doesn't need *your* help in this regard."

"He has a point," Dena said beneath a cloak's hood, taking the ale from my hand as she appeared at the table. "But it is kind of you." She bent over and kissed my cheek, turning to dance away.

"Did you?" I turned, startled, to my compatriot. I'd not noticed her arrival until she was upon us.

"I did not," he laughed, "but am entirely intrigued. You found yourself a lively one, dear boy." He raised his ale in a toast I was now unable to return.

I made to follow her flitting path but was stopped short by a man in a feathered cap.

"Stay," he said, hand upraised. "That's the last you'll see." Ominous hardly began to describe the man blocking my way. A shade above average, with unkempt black hair peeking from beneath his hat, he wore a devilish smile. His bearing and posture spoke of good-natured charm belied by the fire in his eyes.

"I beg pardon," I'd said to him. "Who might you be, and who might she?" I couldn't help but ask the last. Hungry as I was to know her. I felt it in my withered soul every time around.

"The lady is not of your concern," the man said. "I protect her. Mostly from herself," he muttered that bit under his breath.

I didn't know what I knew then, only what I observed. A ghost behind my own eyes. And my observations said not to test this man, not yet. But I knew I'd soon be up for the challenge.

Years passed into another pub and another city, and my friend the Count itched to play his violin. His skill unsurpassed of the time, he should have command performances for kings and queens as befitted his talent. But I'm a bit biased.

So here we sat, waiting in a pub for the bard to be done with his tale.

It was a fanciful one with dragons and kings. And a sorcerer who bound them both to an oath so strong, it outran death itself. The poor dragon. Alone in the castle after the king's demise and the king's sons' and grandsons' as well until only the dragon abided.

"It's like the elephants at the circus," St Germain said, a note of pity filling his voice as he looked at me. "Bound from birth, all they know is the chain. Even though once grown their magnificent strength could break such paltry bindings with ease, they won't try to leave."

Because they don't believe it can be broken, I said in my head. I knew the parable.

"What's a circus?" my old self asked instead. I felt my eyebrows draw up quizzically. How did I not know what a circus was?

"I'm up!" St Germain hopped to his feet, declining an answer to my then-question, grabbing his case and heading to the stage.

"Knock 'em dead," I'd said, or something to that effect. I was still mulling over the circus lack. Words mattered little in memory, less so than sentiment. Something tickled my mind at that, but it could wait — this was his moment to shine after years of toil.

I was proud of my friend. He deserved every ounce of adulation for a feat none could know.

He had finished his task, carefully crafting a most elegant mechanism hidden within a slightly plain brass box. I'd had to talk him out of grand ostentation, much to his annoyance and counter to his givings — reminding him that this was a *hiding* place, not a showcase.

The most vexing part of the whole operation was sundering his payment — one stolen hour from one stolen day — from the remaining twenty-three. That, he compressed into a hiding spot not even I was privy to. But I had my suspicions.

I watched the soon-to-be-immortal alchemist take the stage, withdrawing a plain wooden violin from its case. Decidedly not-ornate and quite un-St Germain, it was still well-crafted and made a succulently sweet sound when he drew his bow.

And then she walked in. Properly dressed this time, a true lady. The crowd hushed as one obviously noble was in their midst. She really couldn't help attracting attention wherever she went.

Never one to be upstaged, the Count enamored the crowd once more with the enchanting melodies he played. Transporting their cares away as if they'd never been. All eyes returned to his slender form as he swayed in transcendent song — save for mine and those of another.

The seat beside me, formerly occupied by my friend, filled with a familiarly ominous presence, distracting from the elegance on display.

"Well hello," the devilish charmer said low. "Fancy seeing you here," he smiled. "No, don't get up." He settled in, sliding a dagger to my side. "We're all just here to enjoy the music."

"The lady included?" My eyes travelled from him to my future wife. Her attention locked to the stage where the violin played. She smiled, entranced.

"The lady especially," he waved to where she sat. "She demanded to hear your friend play. And who am I to say no?"

"Who are you indeed?" The me I'd been'd had much time to study in the intervening years and now knew a devil on sight. This one seemed peculiarly *more* than the others.

"That'd be telling. He's become quite famous, you know," he changed the subject. "Very talented. He make any deals?"

"None that I know," I lied. "Not with your sort." That part was true.

He turned and smiled. Predatory.

"And you?" He couldn't help himself. No devil could once the subject was broached.

"I haven't," I said, "but I might be willing." Time to bargain.

"Tell me now," he leaned closer, dagger digging as his head tilted slightly to the side, "what would you want?" He made no mention of price. His charming smile disarming even as he was armed.

"I think you know," I nodded toward the Lady Dena.

"That is not mine to give," he said, somehow lying and yet not. "You're not good enough anyway," he sniffed derisively at the idea.

"Wanna bet?" I smiled. I knew where this was going. Where it always went. I felt the rush of it each time as if it were the first. "Just a chance to talk," I said harmlessly, "wagered against my soul." I pulled out a coin. "And mine is tastier than most," tempting the devil.

I knew he'd take my bet — I saw it in his hungry eyes.

"And then, I gave him the coin," I told Dena on our first date. First of many. "The look on his face..." I'd squeezed back tears at the telling.

"Poor Haimirich," she called her devilish protector by his old name — not the diminutive I knew him by — laughing affectionately. The melodic sound balmed my weary soul. "He tries so hard."

"It's the deal he struck," I shrugged. "Each time I come call, I wager my soul. Not my fault I never said I wouldn't cheat," I winked at her.

"You're horrible," she pretended to be scandalized.

"You're worth it." I gently held her hand, locking my eyes with hers. She blushed.

"I can see you whenever I want, right?" A wicked glint filled her eye as she took my hand. "I just have to ask?"

"Now who's horrible?" I teased her, then and always after. That, too, had been a part of the deal — he couldn't deny her anything.

We kissed in the moonlight, losing myself in her lips for the first time.

I was in heaven but I had the strangest feeling I was forgetting something.

Something important.

In the distance, I faintly heard church bells ring.

How's Vegas? I baited, trying to draw Felix into conversation. *Put a nickel on red for me!*

Nothing. No dice. No dots. Nada. I had no clue where he actually was, and that was only half the problem.

If you don't respond in ten minutes, I'm coming after you Felix Chance. I sent the threat, unread like the rest, and tossed my phone in frustration.

You know I will, I didn't send.

I'd been updating Felix via text for the last month or... well, three. Halloween didn't seem so long ago, but Thanksgiving had given way to Christmas and New Year's, and now even that was slipping by too fast.

Most people would think he'd ghosted by this point — or actually was a ghost. But I got the feeling I'd know if he were *dead* — if he could be, I'd begun to doubt. Too many signs pointed to 'No' in that regard.

"I'm going after him," I declared to no one in particular, wringing the bar rag I'd been futzing with. "I'm going after him," I said it again, nodding my head for emphasis. My shadow shook its own — rippling and stretching as I got my pack, ever nearby. Old habits, I never knew when I'd need to bolt.

It blocked my way. Arms crossed. Defiant.

"Move." I squared off with my shadow — hand on hip, pack hitched high.

Again, its head shook, arms spread and stretching so it could loom. Rude. My own shadow was against me. I hopped to one side, it followed. I hopped to the other, it went low, tangling my legs until I fell with a clatter.

"What's with the racket," Hank poked his head in. "Oh," he assessed, seeing my shadow-wrapped limbs, pack spilling over the floor. "Stay put." The old devil disappeared.

"Tell her she can't go." Hank had fetched St Germain. I'd learned that, as owner of the Last Chance, I was afforded certain latitudes among the staff — which apparently included Hank, now. Devil Emeritus? Assistant Manager? — such as, they couldn't tell me what not to do and certainly couldn't forbid me from doing anything.

St Germain wasn't an employee. Stupid loophole. Sometimes I thought that was the only reason Hank let him stay.

"Apparently, you can't go, young lady," he said, a bit befuddled. I don't think he'd been awake when Hank conscripted him. "Are you trying to go? Why?" Bushy white eyebrows wiggled higher.

"Because," I succinctly said, disentangling from my shadow. I gathered my lost shit — in every sense of the word — determinedly ignoring the two.

"Oh, *because*," St Germain turned to Hank, "because," he repeated, lips puckered. "Sure, g'head." He threw his hand in the air. "Make like a tree and leave. You won't get ten feet." The alchemist hit my pressure points and rolled his eyes.

I glared. He wasn't wrong, but he didn't have to be so smug about it. I'd need to find a way to leave the Last Chance without Felix's help — and get more than ten feet — if I was going to find the vanished asshole.

"Fine." Not happy, was I. But I had other things to worry about, apparently, if Evette's distressingly pale face was any indication.

"She seeks him. Calls to him."

"To what good? She cannot leave."

"Still," the other timekeeper frowned within the hood. "She has a way of…"

"Chaos," another finished.

"Indeed," the timekeeper agreed, "she feeds into him as he feeds into her."

"How?!" One silent until then slammed a fist down. "Their meeting was not meant."

"And yet…"

"Chance," the finisher finished, wry turn present upon the speaking lips.

Not of Your Heaven

REDEMPTION LIES PLAINLY IN truth. Neither of these have I ever sought, nor will I — undeserving of one, chafingly fettered by the other.

I remember now.

"You can't have her," Haimirich Hank surled my way. Already five fingers deep in drink. Not his favorite, Crown — wouldn't be in business for a while yet — but we still had our whisky.

"That's for the lady to decide," I smiled. He grumbled. "And the fates," I held up a coin, waggling an eyebrow.

"Oh no," young Hank near snarled, "not this time, ya cheat. No coin." He seemed a might sore after our last bet.

"What then?" I spread my palms, open to suggestion.

"Lemme think," he sipped his whisky.

"Why are you so protective of her, anyway?" I'd asked before, to no answer. "She's not kin," I said, "and she doesn't owe you her soul, near as I can tell."

"Owe her mine," he laughed, the whisky loosening his lips. "Hers is unsullied. New." I squinted my eyes at the devil, not interrupting. "Potent." He drained his dram and poured another. "Cult tried to kill her," he fumed. "Sacrifice."

"Who?" His anger infectious, my own hackles rose as my voice went flat. Who'd dare? I'd end them.

"Sons-a-bitches wanted power," he sidestepped the question. "Got me instead." And there it was. Black aura emanated from Hank, coalescing into pure malice and hatred at the memory of violence. My bowels clenched in sheer reflex — still clench, seeing it again.

Guess Hank beat me to it. *Good on ya*, I mentally toasted the devil. His switch flipped back affable.

"I got a baby." Hank's face brightened a smidge. "What was I supposed to do with that?" He drank.

"A good job, apparently," I raised my glass. He eyed me sideways.

"You talk a lot."

I did talk a lot.

Hazard of my occupation.

Gambler, thief, shuckster, conman — if there was a way I could trick some coin, I'd done it.

Usually people who could afford it — I do have *some* scruples — but idiots as well. Especially pompous ones. Have no qualms about reallocating their coin — seems I never have. Thought drifted to the time I stepped in to help this old man sell his parsnips.

"One for three, three for ten," I'd cried in the bustling market — not exactly sure when it was, but some time wearing my third face. He'd looked to be about sixty, but more likely a hard forty at the time — I'm terrible with ages, almost as bad as names. "Heck of a deal!" I'd hawked his veggies with a cheery face while the poor man rested.

One particularly smug-looking mark came up and ordered one parsnip and a beet.

"Thank you and blessings," I said, taking his money. The would-be clever man suppressed a smile as he returned the blessing.

Time slogged on with few customers come call. The old man *had* set outrageous parsnip prices, but my part was to move them regardless.

I began acting a fool to draw the crowd — juggling rutabagas, or were they turnips, and radishes, and the occasional misshapen spud. The kids loved it, the adults liked that I distracted the kids — a couple handing the man some groats — but mostly, it was just for fun.

A nervous woman ordered one parsnip and a bundle of radishes.

"For soup, I suppose?" I engaged in disarming chitchat, running off script. "Excellent combination." I smiled at her genuinely. She averted her eyes — her shame my confirmation. I'd seen her in conspiracy with my mark down the way.

Sir Pompsalot — as I thought of the pompous donkey — strode toward my borrowed stall, now wearing a cap, looking ever so smug.

"One parsnip, please." He handed me the three coins it cost.

"Can I interest you in anything else? I have some radishes left and fine yams," I said, displaying the produce with a flourish. "And, if you fancy more parsnippity goodness, I'm running a special today, three for ten," I drew him into conspiracy — as if I were only offering this fine customer an outrageously good deal.

He suppressed a bubble of laughter. "No, no. Thank you. Just the one parsnip for three, please."

"Fair be it," I said, handing him his produce. "My thanks and blessings." I gave him what I'd now describe as my customer service smile.

"You're terrible at business. Do you recognize me?" the smug mark asked, pulling the cap from his head. By his tone, I suppose it was meant as a disguise? There wasn't a handy name tag, but still, I can recognize a person wearing a cap.

"I bought one parsnip earlier, then another by proxy, and the one just now for a total of three for *nine!*" His moment of boast had driven the giggles he'd failed to suppress. "Not ten, one less than your 'special.'" Derision dripped from his sneer.

"Your math truly adds up," I complimented him. "But you have been a good customer. For that, I thank you."

"Don't you get it? I outsmarted you!" The arrogant prick beamed, cementing my lack of guilt at the exchange. "I got three for nine!"

"Yes, and to teach me a lesson, you also purchased a beet and a bundle of radishes." His jaw slackened. "All for fifteen. So, thank you. Next customer," I dismissed the pompous ass while the old man smiled, counting his new coin.

I'd drifted again, loose behind the eyes. Coming back to Hank, cups down on the table. I knew we were playing Devil's Dice again, as we had so many times to come.

I knew I'd lost, too.

When the cups came up, I'd lose my shot at Dena, lose my winning streak, and flat lose my soul. I honestly wasn't sure which notion rankled me more — probably Dena.

Couldn't have any of that, so I did what I always do. I cheated.

It wasn't until I started reliving my lives that I really understood *how* I did it — it'd just always come naturally to me. I could never tell if I had nudged reality about, if I was mucking with the threads of fate, or if I simply had quick hands — acting on instinct.

I'm just lucky like that. Until I've lost, I can always win.

And I don't lose.

Granted, sometimes it's easier than others. Like when I have ... the smile of a white-haired woman flashed in memory. Who? She cracked open chaos to ease my cheat.

The devil called my name then, drawing me back from the missing memory. Distracted, I missed what I'd done.

Hank made it hard to cheat, watching my every move from a dozen different ways and planes, but it only took the slightest opening to grab the slimmest chance.

I smiled, revealing the Devil's Own — six pips showing on each of the three dice.

"Of all the…" Hank briefly flashed his inner darkness before regaining his composure, running his hand back through his hair. "She wouldn't like it very much if I killed you," he glared at me. "So I guess you win this one."

"Kind of you," I smiled, knowing he couldn't — simply saying it as an open threat. He cared.

"You'll find her in the tree," Hank grumbled around his tumbler, shooting back the amber goodness. "She's taken a fondness to that rock."

"Delightful." That was our spot. I could have guessed she'd be there and gone around Hank. I'd avoid risking my soul, but I'd given my word.

Besides, what fun would that be?

I walked the path I'd re-walked a dozen times by now, careful of every foot-turning stone and snagging root — more familiar now than ever from staring at her painting — but this was new.

A cloying dreadness lay about, I could feel. This hadn't happened in my admittedly spotty recollection, nor been a part of any scene in the painting. The wood had darkened to nightfall though it was only just past noon — Hank abided no clock for his libations — and had grown somehow thicker.

Ah fuck. I don't like it when new things pop up in my own head.

My lips started whistling a familiar tune, finishing it off with a *You'll see.*

Double fuck.

Stone split the air where my head had been, crashing through the undergrowth behind — thankfully, I ducked aside on instinct.

"A kindness if ye please," scritched a familiar voice. "In return for my very favoritest stone, that was." The Bloodybell Bill o'deSoul stepped to the path, palm splayed up, wicked grin splitting cracked lips to show bone-yellowed teeth.

"Not now, goblin," past-me shooed the murder-hobo away. "I've no time for this." Walking by, I smelled the tang of blood soaking his cape.

Goat feet danced nimbly closer — far too close — as the knife-like fingers splayed again.

"Not my fault you caught not my precious gift that now lies crunching amongst the leaves," the red-cape prevaricated. "A kindness if ye please."

Upon unwillingly close inspection, his swept-back horns had taken a purplish hue, and his eyes those of goats to match.

"I asked for nothing," I'd said, "and I'll give nothing. That your rock lies misspent is entirely upon you."

Oh, he didn't like that as I strode past, turning my back. Exactly what the song said *not* to do.

"Fiend and coward to ignore a kindness asked," it spat, lunging with claws outstretched.

I'd turned too late, as it landed on my shoulder, stabbing in for purchase. Murder in his eyes as they met mine, ungainly weight toppling us to the ground.

This wasn't supposed to happen.

Pinned to the ground as I was, he looked through my eyes and into my soul.

"Oooh hoo," he nearly giggled. "We have a guest I see," the murder-hobo tittered. "And who be ye?"

I said nothing, fearing he could truly see my voyeuristic self, and waited for the wound to burn. I ripped the frenzied thing away by its bloody red cape — ick squishing between my gloved fingers. Rising, I hauled the noxious thing higher, internally wincing in anticipation of pain from the stabbed shoulder.

And then...

Nothing. The wound had never been.

"You would assail under the guise of retribution for slight," I'd said, formal and hard, "and bend custom to your wanton bloodlust. For your *kindness*, a curse," I leveled my eyes with his, twisting in my grip. He squirmed as I spoke the barbarous words best not repeated, stripping something from the Bloodybell in the process. "Thrice spoke, and done," I finished, flinging him to the ground.

I wonder if that's the same murder hobo I met...

When?

Something plucked the memory as it formed. The harder I tried to remember...laughter and guts? Of a pumpkin?...the more I was grasping sand. I felt the moments slide from my fingers to skitter down the funnel glass.

"What am I doing here?" I asked from inside, trying to talk myself through it as my legs trod a new path through the oppressive dread."Maybe speaking will call," I said to no one, solidifying my thoughts.

"I'm riding around in my noggin, looking for..." *memories of my lost wife,* I tried to finish. But that was wrong.

I'd come here with another purpose, and Dena's smile kept distracting me. I saw it again, flashing bright in my mind as her lithe limbs reached.

"Deja vu," I triple-took.

"All over again?" Dena laced her arm around my shoulders, pressing against me for the umpteenth time.

"No," I said, pulling away. "For the first time, I see clearly." Her face twisted, eyes narrowing to slits.

The scene transposed, and she sat on the stone statue's head, blank eyes watching the sun set. The tree singed crimson over her head. The stars lost their shine.

I didn't remember this. I'd never seen this...this...sheer desolation of the soul. I screamed inside only to be drowned out by the crows cawing bloody murder in the trees not aflame.

This was later. Lifetimes later.

An older Hank slugged me — slight bend to his back beginning — and I didn't take it. Not even a flinch as he broke his hand.

"You sum-bitch." He grabbed my stunned self with his less broken hand. "Straight to her!" He was sputtering in anger. Black rage flowed from him, impotent as it was turned from my listless form. "You led them!"

They'd followed me, I knew. One of the bubbles, not a repeat. This was my fault.

"I'll get her back," I took a dead tone. "I've done it before."
Dead inside. "I'll do it again." Memory ached to be released.
Memory not of myself.

"Don't you get it, old son?" Tears shone in the devil's eyes.
"Your tricks won't work for her. She's not of your heaven."

*

*"Breaking free!" One of the hooded keepers buckled, clutching a
splitting head.*

"Why'd you go and show him that?"

"He was drifting back to Chaos," the keeper whispered in defense.

*"So you pissed him off!?" The other threw up hands in
exasperation. "You're supposed to distract him with the sexy bits."*

"It wasn't working..."

*"He stopped poking at the cracks," a third keeper entered, "that's
all that matters."*

Garth's hurt, Felix. Something got him. Others, too. We need you.
I didn't know what else to say. He'd left me in charge, and
now people were getting got.

Things were bumping closer in the night, and Garth had
stepped in — protecting a wayward soul harried at the heels
— taking a fang or claw — something pointy — to the
shoulder.

No one got a good look at it — not the traveler, not Garth,
nor any witnesses — and there honestly wasn't much left
after Garth laid hands. But the damage was done.

People were scared. Poor Evette was wracked with nerves
— I don't think she'd ever seen Garth hurt before. Hank

sputtered frustration, gripping his case. Garth had refused the music. The typical crowd — noticeably dwindled of late — muted. Thirstier than normal, but in that drown-your-sorrows kinda way, not the ebullience I'd come to expect from the joint.

Guilt gnawed at me. I should have taken Deirdre's Christmas fright more seriously instead of dismissing her unease as a city girl unaccustomed to a dark wood. They could be terrifying had you not grown up beneath the canopy's shadow. But maybe I'd been wrong. Perhaps whatever she'd encountered hadn't been flashing mucosal membranes as a sign of friendship after all.

"Don't need it, Mr. Hank," Garth wrenched his slinged shoulder away from the fussy fingers probing it. "You save that for those'n that do, please sir."

"You do too need it," Hank insisted, standing on the rungs of his stool so he was near to eye level with the bouncer. "Tell him, Missy." He turned to me for backup. He wasn't going to let this go.

"He's a grown ass...man, Hank." I tried to hide the pause, still not sure quite what Garth was. "He can be a mule-headed lout if he likes." I shrugged and left them to bicker.

I had other problems to deal with.

Namely, the gnomes. Cypnir, Snorkir, and Gnilydbert.

"Bert," I started at the top. "What'd you drag through my door?" The gnomes had taken it upon themselves to patrol after Garth had been hurt. All part of their job, they said — hunting bumpers.

Between them, they'd trussed up one of the bumps and presented it proudly — much like a cat with a kill. But this one still wriggled.

The bundled bump mmrumphed.

Cypnir — or was it Snorkir? They were twins — pulled the hood off the goat-horned head. My eyes widened in recognition.

"You!?" I crouched down close to the creature from the maze. "Come for more coin?" I glared.

The murder-hobo mrumphed again in protest, trying to wriggle his stabby-hands free.

Snorkir — or was it Cypnir? The other one at any rate — thumped the Bloodybell with a mallet. I did remember Felix calling it that — after he'd admitted I hadn't delusioned it.

Stabbykins stilled, though rage boiled in the slits of his eyes.

"Was there anyone," I paused, remembering Stony Meadow, remembering the Byron, "or any*thing* with him?" I glanced up at the gnome hunters, each looking at the other, shaking their beardy heads after conferring.

"No miss, no other bumpers we saw," Bert confirmed. "Just this 'un." Bert put a boot to Bill's ribs. Bill o'deSoul, I believe he'd named himself. The last I'd seen him, he'd been accompanied by things with too-many eyes that looked like cute foxes. And before that...

That memory was hazy. I'd seen the little fox — totally adorable — sprint from the lifted bucket at the Byron and into the deep shadows. I never told Felix exactly what I saw because I wasn't *exactly* sure myself. There are a lot of strange things in the wide world — I was one of them — but I wasn't too familiar with this side of weird. My brain sure as hell was trying to put this guy deep in that darkness, though, watching and smiling as Felix hoisted me and ran.

"Bite me and suffer." I leaned close to the murder-hobo, crinkling my nose. His breath reeked even through the gag. For good measure, my shadow's hand wrapped round his throat, tightening. He glared, not daring to twitch as I freed his mouth.

"I've come for no coin," the Bloodybell spat clear of the rag. "I've come for the bloody charlatan's heart."

The Price of Iron

GOLD OPENS ANY DOOR, even the fake shit. This I learned from the patron saint of perennial houseguests — St Germain. But I wasn't the only one.

I first encountered La Poule Noire behind one such door — installed in the household of a right pretentious con-woman going by the name of Comtesse de La Motte who, in turn, had installed herself in the residence of a right lascivious Cardinal by virtue of shenanigans. The Comtesse leveraged the eighteenth-century equivalent of a sex tape — or maybe sexting was the apt comparison. Either way, she had the screenshots — involving a right bougie, beheaded Queen.

Well, that part would come later.

At the time, this particular chicken was a fledgling, having learned enough parlor tricks to make a name amongst the hoi polloi — the most famous being a gimmick involving plucking a golden egg from the black-feathered ass of a hen, hence the moniker.

And as does everything that glitters, it attracted certain attentions despite not being real gold — the Black Pullet hadn't learned that trick yet. Not until the fateful encounter with the thrice great...I'm getting ahead of myself.

"Bravo, well done." The bemused Cardinal hosting this Hylic strewn garden party clapped politely. He was empty like the rest — I felt distasteful bile rise in my gullet — no soul to speak of. Not one of any worth. "You see, my good people, this conjurer works miracles," the Cardinal said, holding the golden egg high.

The Pullet preened in the adulation. Promising far greater than could be delivered — all toppling soon.

"And thus, through these, France shall be saved from debtors' ruin," pomposity trailed off, leaving behind the Hylics and their grasp at feigned salvation, knowing that soon the ruse would be unmasked and that door would close swiftly on the chicken's ass. I drifted to another door, another place.

This particular door led to a dark, deep wood — eventually, but we're not to that part yet.

While this was not one of those garden party doors, it, too, opened to the press of gold — real gold. These folk knew the difference.

"Just a moment," Fazil the cobbler called around a mouthful of nails. The sound of tapping followed. He must have just been finishing a sole.

I busied myself looking about the shop, taking in the smells of fine leather and shoe polish. Warming myself by the fire, I noticed an oddity. Beside the hearth, set into the mantlework, was a small door around which was set a table and chairs — all seemingly sized for a child. One mug steamed...

"For their break time," the shoemaker said, sneaking up behind me. Soft boots.

I had no idea what he was talking about — did he employ children? Child labor *was* a thing back then. Evidently, my past self knew and carried on.

"Kind of you to provide," I'd said. "Are they about?"

The cobbler quirked his bushy white eyebrows.

"You know I handle their business," Fazil said. "They don't much like people."

"I'm not in need of shoes," I'd said, "though those are remarkably quiet." I paused, considering the cobbler's boots. Finely crafted of supple brown leather. Not ornate, but still, they radiated quality.

"What then?"

"I need to know who made these." I withdrew a pair of fine gloves from my coat pocket. Small and nimble, made for quick fingers by quicker. The supple green leather was stitched along the sides with threads of gold and marked with a fox inside the cuff — a maker's mark? The first two fingers of each tipped with speckled pink.

Fazil frowned, reaching to touch the pair.

"Stop!" A small voice cried from the back of the shop, stopping the old man short. "Don't touch. Bad touch." Soundless feet carried the small man dressed in a red vest, with boots to match, from his hiding spot.

"Bad touch," another small voice echoed behind the mantlework door, carved cleverly with a tree. The owner of the mug — I presumed — snatched open the door and scurried out. Similarly dressed, I could see his features better. Ears swept back on his hairless head, his nose tapered to a point above a black goatee.

They placed themselves between the offending gloves and the cobbler — their caretaker — nearly hissing, drawing their lips back to reveal sharpened teeth, pale skin crinkling like a paper bag. I didn't recall having ever seen such creatures though memory tugged as my past self withdrew a gold piece for each.

"For your troubles." I knelt, presenting the coins to the small cobblers.

Their beady eyes stared into mine, then snatched the gold. I wagered they were nearsighted in my head, likely used to working finely close in the dark.

The first bit his piece, tucking it away in his vest pocket. The other dipped his in his mug, not-so-unlike a biscuit, and took a full bite.

"Tasty," he beamed. "That there's the genuine Aurum." He chewed some more, sipping from his mug of tea. "You interrupted my break, but my thanks for the snack."

"You're welcome," I replied. Courtesy carried much weight. "I'll pass your compliments on to the chef. Your reaction tells me you know these?" I held the gloves forward again, my eyebrow raised in question.

"Bad touch," the first said again. "Death to the living."

"Life to the dead," the snacker added around another Aurum bite.

"No dead here," the other glared, suspicious of me. He had a fair point.

They broke into a fluid chatter — arguing, I'd guess, by the body language. The language was unfamiliar to me, but it sounded like the babbling of a brook, at times rising to the roar of rapids.

The first stormed off, taking the cobbler in tow, leaving me with the one who'd snacked on my gold.

"Don't mind Dain," he said, pointing with the whiskers of his goatee. "Overly cautious sort. Especially with Fazil."

"Understandable, Orym," I'd said, calling him by name. "The world is full of those who would do harm." Bitterness dripped from my voice. I knew that all too well.

"Where you get these?" He wouldn't touch the gloves either, but at least he hadn't shut me out.

"A gift," I skirted the truth. And they were, just not to me.

"Fine gift," his tone full of disbelief. "Gloves from the Fair Folk," he appraised, leaning closer — never too close — and inspecting with a jeweler's eyepiece. "See this stitching?" He pointed to the tiniest of the seams.

"Yes, I'd suspected as much," I'd said. "But who among the Fair? Can you tell?"

"Well," Orym considered. "Not as such. The fox there isn't their mark; it's custom for the receiver." He gave me a look as if I should know that, being the proper recipient I wasn't. "One off."

"Can you make their like? Or your brother?" I ignored the thinly veiled accusation, slight edge of desperation agitating my calm. "These will not work for me."

"No." Orym's answer was flat. Neither he nor Dain would touch the gloves or replicate their touch. "But I can give you a deal on some soft riding boots you'll be needin'." A smile split the hairs on his face, revealing the predatory teeth. He was hungry for more gold. "How you not dead? Holding on to those," he said appraisingly.

Bells rang close. I looked for a clock — distracted from answering.

"What time is it?"

My head swam as the bells rang on.

Another 'friend' of yours dropped by. FYI, he wants to murder you. Running thread still unread, but I had to try. I needed to vent a little and Felix's silent ear was my safest outlet. I couldn't quite trust the others.

Not yet.

I'll give you three guesses who!

Nothing.

I'd snapped a selfie with the restrained Bloodybell, Snorkir and Cypnir sitting on his back for good measure and sent it. Maybe that'd get a response.

Nope.

How'd you piss off the murder-hobo this time? That had been an interesting conversation.

Turns out Bill *wasn't* what wounded Garth or what was stalking the woods. He'd just turned up looking for Felix like the rest of this lot.

You're real popular, you know. I kept hitting send. *Seems like everyone who's shown up since you left me here* — I wasn't bitter about it — *knows you somehow.* At least the ones who made it through, I didn't add.

I had a bad feeling there were a lot of lost souls who never made it to my door. Those that did, didn't want to leave, either.

Except Bill o'deSoul. He wanted out. His prey wasn't here, so he had no further interest. I could empathize.

Might kill you myself when I see you. I sent it teasingly. Winky face and everything.

"Like, sorry to bother," Deirdre chimed in, breaking my trance. I'd been perched on the bar, staring at my phone. "How do you get signal here? I've totally got no bars."

I shrugged. I just did.

"Cool." That had obviously not been what she'd wanted to say. "So anyway," she went on, "I did a pull you need to see."

"Alrighty." I hopped off the bar I'd been buffing with my butt. "Whatcha got?" I expected her to show me her phone or something, but instead, she led me to a corner booth where Hank and St Germain waited.

"Ah, young lady, you need to see this," St Germain welcomed me.

"So I've been told," I laughed, albeit a bit confused. Deidre said she'd done a pull, but no cards were on the table. "Where's this spread?"

"Just watch, Missy," Hank grumbled.

Deirdre sat on the pleather bench, placing the deck on the spread silk cloth before her. In she breathed, and out. *Cleansing,* I thought.

"Ancestors, spirit guides, angels. What is it we need to know? Make it clear, make it clear," she said as she shuffled the tarot.

I was about to ask what was going on when the alchemist held a finger up for silence. This must be important if even *he* was being quiet.

Two cards flipped out together. Followed by a third, then fourth.

The Fool landed upright, obscuring the Magician — peeking out from behind. Then the Hermit sideways and the eight of swords.

"Again!" St Germain exclaimed. "That's the fifth time, young lady," he enlightened me.

"Blast," Hank grumbled again, surliness drawing his arms tight across his chest.

"I was focusing on Felix when I drew the first time," Deirdre explained.

"Okay," I went along, waiting for more.

"These two come up together." She held up the Fool and the Magician. Major arcana. Innocence, free spirit, new beginnings meant the Fool. Manifestation and willpower for the Magician. It was slightly turned toward illusion, though.

"That fits the boy," St Germain said. Hank nodded. I shot a look their way.

"Searching for truth. Inner guidance." She fiddled with the Hermit, upright. "Lost and isolated." She turned him down again.

"Then a trap." She pointed toward the person bound and blinded between crossed swords. I didn't like that card.

Before I could say anything, she swept up the cards, carefully placing the Fool and the Magician in separate parts of the cut, and shuffled again.

"Ancestors, spirit gui—" she didn't even finish when the two arcana popped clear again, "—des, Angels…" she didn't break stride. "What…" another popper, lost, landing sideways, "do we…" and the trap.

"Every time?" I looked around the table at the seer, the devil, and the alchemist. Each nodded in turn.

"They've made it clear," St Germain said at last.

"The boy's in trouble," Hank added.

"Trapped." Deirdre held up the eight of swords.

I looked down at the lack of responses and tried calling instead.

I was that desperate.

The harmonies played a wonderful symphony as we danced by the light of the full moon. The night was alive and so was my love.

Dena looked radiant in the moonlight's silver glow as I swept her around the clearing, our feet barely disturbing the leaves freshly fallen. I couldn't believe I'd found her again. My heart burst with joy.

It wasn't her face — the first having passed nigh two decades ago — but it was her soul. Of that, I was certain.

Hank sat a stump, playing his fiddle as we twirled and rejoiced. I still wasn't good enough for his baby girl, but I was at least better than the rest — he'd let me play for her hand once again, clueing me in to her revival. Doubt the devil would have done that had he not liked me on *some* level. Around him, a band of shadows joined in, creating the sweetest sounds.

The brisk night wore on as the moon rose higher, wreathed in a glowing ring as it cleared the treetops. We fell laughing to the glade floor, staring into the crisp, clear sky.

These were the moments I treasured. Her smile. Her touch. Gentle and loving.

She turned to me, dead eyes milky white as the flames grew higher.

"Why did you let them have me?" the husk of her voice asked through cracked lips.

"No," I pleaded. "I didn't!" Vile revulsion grew in my stomach. This wasn't happening. Wrong.

"Why?" Her empty eyes pleaded with mine, growing larger and larger as I shrank, curling inward around my guilt.

Lost in their depths, I screamed.

"Good, good," the timekeeper gleed.

"Keep him doubting, keep him weak," another agreed.

"It won't last," a third warned. "He's made of sterner stuff than that, tired though he is." A new voice among them.

They watched, ever wary.

"I'm sorry!" My hand paused over the knob for the cobbler's shop. Feverish sweat beaded my brow. My heart pounded as I tried to orient. Where had I gone?

I knew it had happened, but not the when.

I'd lost her.

It'd been my fault.

I'd failed again. Failed to protect her.

"I always fail." I spiraled again toward the edge, down into the depths of mind.

The door opened, knob turning in my hovering hand.

"What's all the ruckus?" Fazil peered out to see what loon made the fuss. "Oh, you. Come in, come in," he waved, stepping back inside.

I stamped my heel thrice, clearing my mind, rooting in the here and now. I would punish myself later. For now, I needed new boots.

While Orym had refused to make the gloves, he'd clued me in to where they could be found — but I'd have to pay. So much to pay for.

"A price for everything," Dain said.

"And everything for a price," Orym finished, placing the supple boots on the table.

"And what price for these marvelous boots?" Light as a feather, the boots glowed with infused aura and made nary a sound as they'd fallen to the table.

"The price for our craft," Dain held open his palm. "Paid in silver."

I gave him a fat pouch.

"The price of Iron," Orym followed, holding out his hand. "Paid in Aurum."

I fished out more of St Germain's finest, passing it to the two cobblers. Dain, the hungry one this time, snatched his and downed it in two large bites.

"Now try them on," Orym gleefully waved. Eager to see his handiwork in action.

I slipped the boots on and stood, frowning slightly.

"A bit big, aren't they?" I stomped about a bit as the boot tops flopped around my calves.

"Give 'em a minute," Orym grunted. "Need to get used to you. Get comfortable."

"The boots need to get used to me? Not me to them?"

"You got the easy part," Dain said. "You just bumble about like a lout."

"Boots'll figure your step out," Orym added for further obfuscation.

Unsure, I took a few test steps around the shop, and as I wobbled, the boots shrank to fit my feet. So soft, supportive; I'd never felt their like before.

"These are amazing!" I spun as I marveled at their feel, their perfect fit, and yet still they shrank until my feet hurt. "Wait, are they…" I looked at Orym, panicked. He seemed to grow larger.

Turns out the boots didn't just shrink to fit my feet. They shrank me as well. Down to the height of Orym and Dain.

"Come on then," Dain waved me to the tree-carved door, opening it onto a green meadow. "Time to meet the maker."

Ominous much? I stepped forward, slipping past Orym, waiting for me to pass, Dain already on the other side. Up close, I saw the minute detail of his vest — finely embroidered with scenes of swirling dancers. At least, I thought that's what they were. The smaller I'd gotten, the easier it was to see the intricacies where before it appeared a simple paisley pattern.

Where the meadow was full of sunshine and those flowers may as well be lollipops for all I could tell — brightly sworled colors dripping with dew — the edge of the wood grew dim and crinkly as things shifted unseen in their shadows.

"Careful about now, lad," Orym said, hammer slung over his shoulder. Its iron head hissed and sizzled through the very air as we walked — tendrils curling from his hand. He munched on a sliver of gold as we trod to the shadow line, grimacing along the way.

"These're the wildlands and are none too forgiving." Dain walked ahead with an iron-capped staff, crisping the leaves brown in his wake.

Cindering aside, we left no sound as we passed. My new boots muffled all, seeming to turn all the leaves and blades soft in my favor, nary snapping a twig.

There appeared before us a path to take, one where our passage would do no harm — mostly from the cobbler's iron tools. Did we need weapons? I felt woefully unprepared, but knew my former self had many tricks at the ready. To either side of us, the woods teemed with life unseen. Hidden from our eyes by the myriad brush and clutter, yet sounding close to nipping at our toes.

"Quit flinching about," Dain chided me, walking the straight and narrow. "They're doing it a purpose to get at you."

"Best ignore 'em," Orym agreed. "Nasties need no such tricks," he added, "and you'll ne'er hear 'em coming."

Thanks, guys. That wasn't comforting in the slightest. I peered deeper into the shadowed boles, seeking the source of the overly loud detritus and clutter. Some sassy squirrel clod-hopping about, skittering all the oak leaves aside, and throwing acorns for good measure.

So focused on the far, I never noticed the cobblers stop trailing beside me until they called.

"End of the line, boyo," Dain yelled, petting a rabbit by the wayside. Where had it come from?

"Far as we go, anyhow," Orym added, pulling a pipe and seating himself on a fallen log. "Your guide is here," he pointed.

Soundless behind me, there was a sudden goat. An actual goat — not the murder-hobo-halfling-kind of goat — chewing peacefully on stripped bark. The white whiskers on its chin waved about as it ate, head turning sideways to strip another bite. Scrolled horns curled in on themselves atop the goat's skull, forming something resembling overwound clock springs, bulging to either side of its head.

Small as I was now, the goat seemed rather large and imposing. Muscles rippled under its neck and shoulders as it masticated the woody pulp before straying from my previous path.

"Go on now," Dain shooed. "Best keep Hora in sight."

"Who-ra?" The goat was already slipping from sight through the underbrush. I felt odd, ducking under low bushes instead of stepping around. Saplings passing like fully formed boles as I caught sight of the springing horns.

Hora kept an eye on me, making sure I'd followed before jumping to a tree, eating the leaves along the branches — springy horns winding and unwinding, undulating in the motion.

"Are they tastier up there?" There were plenty of other leaves down here. Hora hopped on, branch to branch, nomming as it pleased. Occasionally *maaaah*ing at me if I didn't keep pace. I didn't speak goat, not like...

Hora turned to stare, distracted from the meal. The horns turned and torqued in a hypnotic spiral. The faint sound of bells again... had it been wearing one to graze?

I saw no collar...but the sound...drifted...

They're coming! I texted, furious. *Trying to get in!* No reply. *Goddamit Felix we need you!*

Boards battered again, barely holding over the shattered window. It had all happened so fast...

Hank was down, not moving. The black lump that had flung itself through the plate now decorated the columns and dripped from the ceiling, courtesy Garth's rage. He lashed out with his one good arm as three more bore down on him.

They boiled in through the breach — whatever *they* were. No faces, no eyes, nothing to even say they were alive — suffocating the room.

My shadow tangled and mangled two as I flipped a table for cover, dragging Hank behind. Garth swung his fist surgically, peppering the blobs with his Garthiness until they joined the ceiling goo.

Elder stumbled into the fray, head lowered for a charge, sweeping his massive antlers through the oily forms, sending tables and chairs flying about. They oozed around the velvety rack, trapping him. He slipped and slid in the viscous, going down.

"Elder!" Damnitall, he was still weak from the wolves. I couldn't get to him. Couldn't help him and Hank at the same time. My shadow was busy and I just felt helpless — well out of my league — when a blood red flash zipped to his aid.

"Ooh hoo, what have we," the Bloodybell gleed, skissing his needle-sharp claws. His eyes lit with danger as he began stabbing into the heart of the oily blackness drowning the moose. "Heeeere." His crooked smile bloomed, examining the throbbing mass skewered on his finger till it throbbed no more.

"Who cut him loose?" Just what I needed, a psychotic murder-hobo set free. At least he broke Elder loose from the goo's hold. The giant moose tried to rise, encumbered by masses of blob on his antlers. One great shake of his head solved the problem, shedding them without pause.

"Who cares?" St Germain called from dead center of the fracas. "He's effective!" His hand clutched Hank's precious fiddle case to his chest as he ducked a flying blob and slid home to me. "Is he…" the alchemist trailed off.

"He's breathing," I said, unable to add the *barely*. "But he won't be playing for this crowd." That would make things a lot easier.

"Guess I'm up next then," he stretched his neck. "Been too long." The Count carefully opened the fiddle case, letting the golden light shine forth, searing one of the blobs come too close.

Oh shit. They took notice of that, rushing the immortal.

"Dear girl, do keep them busy a moment?" The alchemist carefully withdrew the fiddle of solid gold from its case, delicately caressing a string with the bow.

The massing darkness closed in, ignoring everyone else. My shadow lashed out, barely slapping the seeking tendrils away. I heard shouting from the other side — likely Garth and the Bloodybell setting into the vileness — but more, I heard the sweet sounds of St Germain.

The way he played the instrument was starkly different from Hank — slow and enchanting — classical violin as opposed to Hank's sawing on the fiddle.

Golden glow suffused the room, bursting forth through the darkness gathered like a blazing sun as the immortal played. St Germain swayed, lost in the music, diamond ear stud glinting in the warm light.

Where this angelic light touched, black goo dissolved, and the bumps concealed in liquid darkness seemed to…heal. Uncorrupted, their original forms took hold, transforming into creatures I'd not seen before, and barely saw then, as they each made for the window to escape as soon as their darkness was dispelled — clearing the room in shambles.

Before more could flow in, my shadow pulled the shutters tight against the regathering blackness as it massed. The lantern flame flared wildly hot blue.

"Mr. Hank!" Evette cradled him in her arms as St Germain cradled the fiddle in turn. "Mr. Hank," she tried to bring him to, shaking him gently. He breathed, at least.

"What are they?" I opened the floor to answers from any that had them. Distant fury raged outside like a storm of darkness swallowing the Last Chance, putting all on edge. I stared at many scared faces.

"Bad news, Missy," Hank supplied, at last coming around.

"Hank!" I crouched by his side. "Don't scare me like that." I touched him gingerly. "Anything broken?" I saw no visible wounds, but it had been a nasty fall. Plus, who knew what effect inky blackness had on a soul. Judging by the maddened creatures freed and fleeing…

"I'm fine," he shrugged us both off. "I'm fine," he repeated, sitting up. "It'll pass," he said.

"What'll pass? What is this?"

Hank ignored the question, rising to stand before St Germain.

"Hope you don't mind," the Count said, holding the bow and fiddle, easy as breathing. "I borrowed it."

"Can't take what's rightfully yourn," Hank gruffed, picking up the case. "'Sides, you still play great."

"It was always my favorite." St Germain smiled, placing the instrument carefully back where it belonged. "You kept it well-tuned."

"'Course I did," Hank laughed. The two shared a glance and turned.

"Any word from the dear boy?"

I checked my phone. Nothing. I shook my head.

"Ah huh," Hank uttered. "Might need him." He turned to the banging shutter, barely holding back the storm.

We were trapped.

BANG my head hit hard.

"Ow, can you...oof..." Hora's hooves clattered against the rock. "Jump...gah...any...burf...more..."

And before I could say *gently,* he leapt to a passing cloud — floating weightless as dream, we rose. Above, brown crags broke through, soaring above the mist.

I'd dazed after I'd gazed at the goat's hypnotically springy horns, coming to on Hora's back as we flew through the air, horns unfurled having sprung — landing on the sheer side of a mountain as they wound again.

I wasn't sure if he'd truly flown or simply flung himself at the ground, only to miss. Whichever it was, we floated along, gentle as a breeze. The cloud was in no hurry.

I think I passed out. Wide-eyed terror? Oxygen deprivation? The likeliest culprits. All I know is I woke up drooling into Hora's fur, clinging on for dear life, tasting the iron tang of blood in my mouth — apparently having bitten my tongue or cheek on the ride.

It was not a flattering way to introduce myself to the Seelie of the Dawn. But I wasn't exactly there to make friends.

"Foolish mortal," one of the guards in lacquered armor started a standard derisive trope. He stood at the ready to intercept would-be interlopers like myself, placed between the figure in the glade beyond and dangers come call.

"Half right," I cut him short, my words hissing in the air. "Remains to be seen which."

Elegant laughter bubbled from the brookside. Someone thought I was amusing. It was a start. Ignoring the guard, I patted Hora, mentally thanking the goat for the bumpy ride as he found an interesting — likely tasty — bush.

"Brash," the melodic voice. "Speaking poisoned words as well," the lady Fair tsked.

"Curr," the interrupted guard bristled, drawing down on me.

"Leave him be," the voice commanded. "I feel no malice and fancy amusement." The speaker strode from the shaded glade. Gossamer silver flowed over her form, dripping from elegant curves.

I could make so many mistakes with her, my present self thought, though past-me reacted not at all.

"Do us, at least, the courtesy of paying the Iron Price as you speak, if you would be so kind."

This confused me, past and present. Orym and Dain had mentioned the Price of Iron, but I had no…

"She means suck some Aurum, bloody-mouthed bastard," the guard finally proved useful.

So *that's* what it meant. I scratched my hand through my hair, twisting a bit about, and pulled more of St Germain's finest from my stash. Popping the coin under my tongue, I hoped I didn't have to swallow.

I pulled two more, offering a bite to my hosts. Only polite.

"We've no need," the gossamer fairy sneered, "for we touch no iron." She ran her hand evocatively over succulent skin. Not withered and cracked like Orym's. "Iron corrupts," the fairy continued. "Those low who would work it pay the price."

I'd never thought about it before, but outcast as they were, Orym and Dain were still among the Fair. To them, the cobbler's tools and trade should be poison.

"And the gold remedies that?"

"In a manner," she nodded. "Now, why have you come?"

"Simple," I smiled, "I seek death."

The Waters of Lethe

THE FIRST TIME I didn't die, I wasn't trying very hard — I'd simply withered away, fragile husk fading only to be replaced by another. I'd gone through two faces like this. By the third...well, they started running together.

Each time I'd crossed, I'd been denied. Left out. Told to go back. I remembered a few of them, though they were still hazy. One thing was abundantly clear — my place in Heaven was forfeit.

I guess that's what I get for making deals with Hank — though that didn't sit quite right according to the itch in my brain.

Regardless, Dena had gone where I couldn't go, which wasn't possible.

Or it shouldn't have been, but the damn Golden Dawn had...

"Happy to oblige." The guard lunged, sword piercing the air toward my neck. I didn't flinch, stone-faced stoic, as the silver blade shattered mid-stab.

A fault in the making? That happened — more often than not around me. The unlucky elf — was he an elf? He was tall, though no pointy ears — recoiled at the unexpected shrapnel.

"My eye," he screamed, clutching. Piss poor luck — a shard from the sword had found the misfortunate mark.

"There you go, getting my hopes up." Sarcasm dripped. I felt a wave of self-disgust — not liking the person I'd become.

"He'll live," the lady Fair tittered. "'Twas not an iron blade." She expressed even less concern than I.

"As it may." I'd stepped past the prone guard, quieter now. Cold. Detached. That's how I now saw my past self. I couldn't really blame him; I felt it, too — the grief and loneliness swirling deep inside. The sleepless guilt that gnawed with sharp teeth — constantly reminding. Never had I felt so detached from... me.

"What business has one so young with death?" Bemusement drew her full lips up in a wicked smile. I looked down at myself — body young, new. I'd honestly forgotten what face I wore — obviously one she didn't recognize. She should? — but I certainly had a couple centuries under my belt by that point.

"Not so young as you may think, Misha," I said, calling her by name. Finally! Honestly, I couldn't wait for handy-dandy name tags to come in vogue. This was some bullshit, always waiting for past-me to address others by name. So damn tired of it. Just get to the parts I need to see already so I can...

Things went fuzzy again. I remembered a curse needing to be broken, but that's as far as I'd gotten. Yes, Dena had been cursed by a cult and I needed to break it. No...it was the Fair Folk...I thumbed for the gloves at my belt.

"*You?*" Misha's already large eyes grew even wider in surprise. She tensed.

Past-me had that effect on people. I don't remember why, exactly. Tend to skip over those bits in the replay.

Like we skipped over the Fair Folk glade...I'd reached for the gloves, only to find them missing — drifting again. Hadn't even noticed that one.

She sat at a bar now. Full-size vixen in a red dress, drinking a Martini and looking deadly. The noise closed in around me.

Realizing where I was, I felt older, much older, and weary to my bones.

"Fancy seeing you here," I'd smiled viciously, sliding onto a neighboring stool. "Whisky, neat," I called to the bartender, looking familiar in her slicked-back do. She, in turn, shot a glance to Misha, no doubt asking if help was needed in not-so-many-words — the lady Fair waved her off.

"No goat this time? Or is the valet parking him?" Daggers shot, ineffective.

"No goat," I laughed. "Have a new ride this lifetime." I'll tell you later.

"How nice," she gave me a tight smile.

"Bouncer still has both eyes, too." I toasted with my newly poured whisky, tipping the tender well.

"Kind of you," Misha said. "To what do I owe the displeasure?"

"Oh, same as last time," I dithered. "Nothing big." I ran the whisky 'round the glass — good legs on this one.

She burst out laughing — not the good humor kind of hahaha, more the rueful kind where you're barely suppressing the urge to stab someone.

"The audacity." She got indignant, her head cocking back, ready to unleash a lashing. I guess others didn't like me either. "You cost us everything, you self-righteous asshole!" Misha made to throw her drink in my face — forgetting the shattered sword still fresh in my memory — only to be bumped from behind, spilling it down her dress as it slipped from her hand.

"Go ahead and change," I said. "I'll wait." I sipped my whisky as she twisted, focusing my eyes distant — only polite not to look.

I felt time tug at me again — that's where I was, right? Stuck. Yes, that felt right — I fought the coming drift. Stronger here, in this place so familiar. Feeling now the deep well inside my past self.

"Told you," Hank said from behind. "Don't be comin' here no more." He still didn't like me — time mends nothing, really — and with good reason. I turned to see Princess looming behind. I'd slipped past him unnoticed at the door, but there was no fooling Hank.

The old devil reached for me with gnarled hand — the one he'd broken on my face — stopping short of my collar. Had he tried to grab it, I don't know what would have happened. I was glad he didn't — I was still fond of Hank even in my then-dead heart.

I straightened a bit, just out of range lest my luck lash out.

"It's good to see you, Hank," I'd said quietly. "For all that means from me."

Hank frowned. "You need to go."

"I do, and will," I'd said. "Last time I'll bother you." Misha twisted back in during the standoff. "Perfect timing," I dead-smiled.

The startled lady Fair looked between me and Hank, wide eyes taking in the fractious air. Gone was the dress, replaced with a more casual and comfortable-looking white sweater — one that draped fashionably.

"Actually," she said, "I think I'll be going." Nervously she backed from the both of us.

"I was just leaving myself," I'd said, "I'll walk you out." My cold tone brooked no dissent. "Before I go, though..." I turned back to Hank. A flourish of my hand fetched a wax-sealed scroll from wherever such things come from, presenting it to Hank in a fluid motion. "Should we meet as friends again."

"'Nother favor?" He raised an eyebrow over his scrunched-up face. "You already owe me."

"And I'm afraid I'll be a while paying you back," I bowed my head. "Should things go well."

"For you," Hank grunted. "They usually do. Everyone else I'm worried about."

I sighed.

"Me too, Hank," I frowned. "Me too."

Clock bells struck the hour, the hands unstuck.

Panic flooded the room.

Save for one, unmoved.

Hank's scaring me, Felix, I swiped out. *It's like he swallowed a bunch of pissed off hornets.* And he wouldn't tell me a damn thing. *Says you know something.*

I don't know why I looked for the dots. They never came. If he was trapped like Deirdre said, he didn't have his phone, but I kept texting anyway.

Please be okay. It made me feel at least a little connected.

It wasn't just Hank, everyone was — rightfully — nervous.

Evette polished glasses that hadn't been served, Garth worked his wounded shoulder, readying for action. Elder rested by the bar, looking decidedly odd without the accustomed antlers.

There had been more attacks — though nothing of that first scale. Ookie blobs slipping through, shying from the light. Each time they targeted me, or...

Hank and St Germain conspired in a corner booth, the alchemist fidgeting with the diamond stud in his ear.

"We need to leave," St Germain was saying. "Find the dear boy." Hank's face was having nothing of it.

"I'll go," I butted in. I'd tried to convince them to let me go before, and if they were budging...

"Bad idea, Missy," Hank dismissed the notion, crossing his arms with finality as only an old man can. He winced, coming close to denying me. "And we aren't leaving you," he looked pointedly at St Germain.

"I can leave," I insisted. "Really. I'll be fine."

"For a moment," St Germain allowed. "But then what? What'll you do when you leave the lantern light and your roots grow firm?"

"Keep making like a tree," I giggled. I'd have to, sooner or later.

"And leave!" Maya poofed into the booth as she fidgeted through forms, popping about the empty bar in wisps and drafts. This time she grew branches from her head, skin turning to bark.

Not quite how it works, dear, I didn't say aloud. St Germain quirked a brow my way.

"No good. Bumps target you," Hank said, "and me."

It made sense. The Last Chance was a refuge built on the will of the owner — past and present. Without either of us, it'd be a feeding ground. Even with one of us gone, if the sneakers found our weakness...

"Not to mention, if you leave, dear girl, you'd be far too exposed," St Germain added. "Vulnerable without the protections provided here."

I frowned, stopping short of full sulk. I wanted to reply I could take care of myself, but they had a point, and I had no counter. There were no good options and it showed.

Even Tony felt to be nervous, nomming on the tables and chairs upturned even though he just ate a whole dumpster — he *was* a growing boy, after all.

The only ones not nervous were the fjøsnisser — used to hunting bumps — and strangely, Bill.

The Bloodybell sat with a file doing his nails, whistling as he went — sharpening each long skewer of a claw to a gleaming point. He saw me looking his way and gave me a bone-toothy grin — elated by the prospect of future violence. Ready to go full murder-hobo again.

Green-haired goth Maya poofed next to me, biting the less-sharp nail of her thumb. The green didn't last, hair sliding through the whole Crayola box — the sixty-four pack. Jealous. I missed being able to do that. My hair was stuck white ever since that traitorous kiss — stupid fairy. Couldn't shift it in the twist and even normal hair dye didn't hold despite being perfectly white — no bleach necessary. I wondered...

"Maya, hon, can you do me?"

I had an idea. Part of one, anyway.

The sun set, gilding the glade in preternatural glow as Misha drew me to her Folk further along.

"We are far, here, from the poison lands where you hail," she narrated like a competent tour guide. All she needed was a lanyard — though that would have clashed with diaphanous nothing she wore so well. Threads of gossamer clung to her like the mist clouds caressing the edges of sight.

Chimes, distant but clear, rang out the hour. Another day passed on into dark — soon, the Night Court would hold sway. A delightfully liminal time to be — the possibilities...the chances...were infinite.

My imagination ran wild as we waltzed through the crowd gathered to celebrate the dusk — any excuse to party for this lot — as I saw fairies flit about in their hazy glow circling ol' Sassy-pants' head — though he knew me not yet to say hello — standing next to a swaying man crowned with stag horns who bumped into a bird as his great helm turned unsteady.

A hawk, to be specific — or maybe an eagle — one who landed with a crackle of irate lightning.

"Watch it, Erl," the bird thundered, its voice deep and distant. Talons turned to feet as it stalked forward, sparks flying from eyes. Wings melded into hands gripping a feathered cloak of bright colors. It threw its head, flipping the beak back as it flipped off the giants.

"Easy, Lenny," Sassy-pants placated the ruffled bird-man. "Erl meant no harm," the big guy said. "Sexy here's just had a few too many." Must have made the mistake of going one-for-one. Damn Sassy, even the supernatural can't keep up? "Let's get you a drink or three, hon," Sassy was saying. "Loosen up that tight..."

I wanted to drop eaves more, but I wasn't in the driver's seat this lifetime — we went on, Misha making vague introductions to folk who did not care. They were there to be seen, to be admired and fawned over. They were there for the attention.

I had other plans.

"You're insane," St Germain said.

"Never said I wasn't." I flipped through my phone for Maya. Syncing all the selfies I'd taken, toks I'd ticked, whatever she needed to play me up with the phone Felix gave her. "Can you make it?" I asked the alchemist.

"Can I copy a priceless one-of-a-kind relic that removes wielders from the flow of time, granting them…" he trailed on as he does.

I'm really grateful for all the times you glossed over StG's windbagginess, I texted Felix. *Didn't realize just how much he went on…and on…and…*

"Of course," St Germain finished at length. "Who do you think I am? That hack, Newton?"

"Sir Isaac Newton?" I was dubious. "Inventor of calculus and…well, gravity?" The alchemist was always dropping names like lead balloons. The heavier, the better.

"Who else? Toss a kid an apple and he thinks he's a genius," St Germain ruffled. "Why that little…" he launched.

"What do you need?" I cut him off before he could tangentialize any further.

"Time," he replied soberly. "I need time." The Count thumbed his stud again, brow furrowed in thought.

Great. I eyed the boarded window, expecting it to burst inward any moment. The lantern light flickered brighter as whatever was outside sought entrance.

"One thing we don't have," I sighed.

"More than you think, but still not enough," St Germain sighed to match my own, disappearing into another room.

"You know where it's at, now," Misha cast disparage my way, descending into the Fair Folk crypt. "Why do you need me?" She shivered, clutching her sweater tighter against the coming chill.

"Because you have the key," I'd said, holding the torch high.

"I wish I'd never met you," she shot, daggers still ineffectual. I'd long since cared not what others thought.

"Most do," I'd sighed. "Eventually."

The air was thick with the scent of earth and — strangely — sweet flowers, remarkably fresh for being so deep within the ground. Black stone pillars framed the round portal to either side, carved with sharp thorns and thick vines that spread across the opening which seemed to writhe as we approached — suspicious of newcomers — sealing the entrance tighter. Mists, black as empty night, gathered to further obscure the way beyond.

"The perfect grave for the living," Misha sneered. The black mists within the portal exhaled as she approached, sending tendrils that smelled of daisies toward her. She hissed, sending them back. "Didn't you get enough trouble last time?"

I certainly didn't get what I wanted, or even what I needed. That's for sure.

"This time's different," I'd said, meeting her eyes. She couldn't look away, so I broke contact first, turning to the portal. "And you don't have to wait," I added.

She frowned, pulling a golden talisman from around her neck, and spoke the Orphic text. Blue ghost flame bloomed in the air, causing the mists to shudder. The black stone brambles caught alight in the spectral fire, burning away as the roiling darkness began to part, revealing lush planes beyond, cut through with three rivers — though I knew there were two more. The door only opened from one side — this side.

"When should I come back for you?" Shadows danced ominously upon her hollowed pale face, cast from the flickering spirits — her true nature revealed.

"Don't." I stepped through, not looking back.

I didn't pry into the cosmic mysteries of the alchemist. Instead, I put the question to Hank while St Germain worked.

"You talked to Felix right before he left," I eyed him, sitting at the table, playing with his drink. "Did he say where?" I'd caught them mid-sentence, both shutting up before I could hear.

"No." Man of many words, our Hank. "Gave him his fancy letter, he left." Simple as that.

"Letter?" Curious.

"Had a green lion on it," Hank nodded. "Wound up real tight and small."

"Yeah," Maya chimed in, "he kept looking at it after..." She grinned sheepishly. Of course Maya had been the last to see Felix.

"He tell *you* where he was going?"

Maya frowned, mirroring me in a puff of smoke. I shivered.

"If he didn't tell you, he certainly wouldn't tell me," Maya huffed. "Just told me to come hide here and gave me that doohickey." She meant the phone she still couldn't read. Somehow stuck and still visible in the lantern's light.

I frowned.

"That and this cocktail recipe," Maya went on. "He stared at that too, even when I tried to distract him." As she spoke, her top cut low — far too low while wearing my face. Just what had she...Nevermind, I don't want to know.

"What cocktail?" I changed the subject quick.

"Don't know, toots. That's what he called it," she leaned back, displaying less of the goods. "All squiggles to me," she soured. "Just said he needed bay leaves."

"Bay leaves!?" St Germain reappeared, looking rather haggard and slightly older. "Sounds like my recipe for Aurum."

Beside him floated a most clever device — a lantern of paper with a metal tray and open flame burning blue.

The party was so far a bust — for my past self, anyway. I was having a blast watching all the Fair Folk cavort and cahoot and other words that sound fun to say. Had it all been so ordinary to me once that I ignored this magic?

My face frowned. Misha had left me to my own devices and I found myself sipping fermented nectar from a tulip — not tulip glass, an actual tulip — large in my hand still shrunken small.

Fairy lights floated about, dispelling the gathering night with their blue glow — a glow that made the shadows sharper and a tad harsh while cherubic skin softened and smoothed ageless. Leave it to the Fair Folk to invent a light that everything looked good in. You could really up your selfie game with such lighting, especially if it floated by the camera and off to the side. Molly'd have a...

MOLLY!

How could I forget Molly? That's why...the fog crept in again, trying to drag me back into the drift. I stomped my booted heel thrice, grounding myself in this moment, place, and mind.

I was here to learn what I once knew. I needed to help her. I needed their help to do it.

My former self and I locked into sync.

We leapt to a stump and flourished a bow, sending up lights of our own to startle this sideshow.

I bit my cheek, tasting the blood tang.

"May I have your attention, please?" I held my hands high, my bloody words spreading like poison. "May I have your attention, please?" I echoed, reminding myself of the most polite yet ineffectual fire alarm I knew. "If I may have your attention, please look to me."

One by one, the conversation dulled as eyes traveled to the fool standing a'stump. All in attendance murmured and whispered, not sure what to make. Each gave a glance, a sliver of thought for the taking. Making contact with all present, my face grew a wicked smile.

"Thank you," I bound them in blood.

I knew I'd just done something monumentally clever, or stupid, but I wasn't exactly sure which. I felt ripples of ramifications spread from the moment, moving forward and backward then and now, but I cared not and carried on.

"Now," they stared enraptured, unable to look away, "let us begin."

The plan is simple enough in that not-so-simple way. Maya will play me, and I'll come find you! Hank has to stay because she

could only play one of us. I filled Felix in on my brilliant plan. *And I'll leave the shadow behind to sell Maya as me.*

The rest was still in question. I wanted to go alone. That didn't fly.

"At the *very* least, I'm coming with," St Germain proclaimed.

"Still say I should go. You stay," Hank grumbled. He had not been too happy I won the coin toss. Even less happy when I insisted we use my coin this time.

"You and your fiddle stay here where you're both needed," I told him for the thousandth time. I didn't know why I *had* to go, but I knew in my bones it had to be me.

"Well, I'm staying here," Maya said resolutely.

We turned and blinked at her.

"Yes dear, that's the entire crux of the plan," St Germain said kindly.

"You should take Garthy-poo, though," Maya added, standing next to the burly bouncer. "May need some muscle."

"He's hurt," I said. "And he won't let Hank heal him," I shot a side-eye Garth's way.

"She's right, though," St Germain spoke up. "We may need some muscle. I'm not as immortal as I used to be," he said with a touch of resignation.

"If those things break in here, they're going to need all the muscle they can get. Garth, Hank and his fiddle, Elder, Bert and the other gnomes. Not to mention my shadow," I said, sending it to sit with Maya. "There's no one else," I said. "We'll just have to not get caught." It was a grim prospect.

We were already wounded, and I had a sinking feeling whoever *they* were, they hadn't shown their strength yet.

"Then take me," Bill o'deSoul bound to a stool, gaining its height. "I'll get you to him safe as a lambkin," he laughed, skissing his sharpened fingertips.

"No," I point-blank refused. "No way I can trust you to have my back." Oh hell no. Just no.

"What deal do you propose?" St Germain countered in earnest. "His kind are good in a fight," he turned to me, "as you've seen. And if he makes a deal…"

"My word binds like iron," the murder-hobo bowed. "I've no quarrel with you, nor with the gilded one…" the hell was he saying … "'tis truly a small price, I say," a vile grin split his face, "just pray let me try feel the trickster's beating heart."

St Germain and Hank exchanged sour looks, then grins as if they saw the same idea dawn.

"To be clear," St Germain took on the old tone, "you'll do us no harm and see us safe in return for a chance to kill Felix?"

"Verily," the Bloodybell sang.

The whole thing was preposterous. How could they even…

"Deal," they said in unison.

"Unholy binds," said one.

"Such is…" a second began.

"…the Chaos flow," the third finished.

"I once stood here in hope," I spoke to the river's edge. "I now stand here with a different hope."

"A hope for what?"

"I can't remember," I'd said, handing back a cup.

"Then it is working," he refilled it from the waters. "Here, drink some more."

I now watched the scene, fully aware, unaffected by the river's touch. I saw a man brought low, weary by the weight of futile struggle. Bowed by the inexorable tide of time, denied rest again and again. I saw the shell that remained, hollowed out by the happiness I'd sought to reclaim — fool that I was. Had I only known...

I'd sought a way to bring back my wife, gripped tight by a fate worse than death. There was none. I'd sought a way to bring her peace. There was none. I'd sought a way to outright cheat them all. There was none.

Now, I simply sought to escape the pain, the loneliness, the guilt caused by my hand.

To be washed clean by the waters of Lethe.

I sought to forget.

Reasons

"COME...COME," THE SHADOWS BECKONED — a voice wisened yet sultry. "Come see your fate in the crystals..." the raven-haired Romani enticed. Kohl-lined eyes flashed bright in the dim tent, her bangled arms glinted in the low candle light as she waved hands sinuously over a faintly glowing orb. "What would you know, weary traveler?"

I smiled, past me and present knew this reader tucked away in the alley mouth. Madame Zestra — ever consummate at plying her trade.

"Hello, Z," I approached warmly. "Good to see you with my eyes."

She paused at the odd statement, no next line at the ready on her lips. Squinting, she leaned closer to see with other eyes. Hoop earrings swayed, clinking against her crystal ball.

"Careful," I stepped into the tent, "wouldn't want to damage your props."

"You?" I'd never known her to be so bereft of words — kind or otherwise. "But you're..."

"Dead?" I supplied with a quirk of my eyebrow.

"I was going to say 'crossed over,'" she recovered, straightening her back and tightening her jaw. "How do you walk among the living?"

"I *was* on the other side last we spoke," I laughed — heck of a long distance call. "But I don't stay very long. Never been properly dead, come to think."

Zestra took the odd answer in stride. She was a spiritualist — medium, psychic, gifted, whatever you wanted to call her — the real deal with uncanny abilities, but... it really wasn't what anyone thought it to be.

Certainly not those dime-museum seances and parlor tricks — you know, the stuff people would pay for. *That* mess truly was for entertainment purposes only. She was good at that, too — could bilk with the best of them. The years between wars were prime for it — so many seeking solace, grieving for the massed dead.

She'd made contact while I moped about Lethe's edge, not yet taking the plunge. I'd dipped my toe in, though, feeling the pull of oblivion's sweet abyss.

'Messages from the great beyond' was the request. Irritating, really. I'd faffed about long enough, though, so I thought I'd see who was calling. Thing was, Zestra never expected anyone to pick up. She was just sitting in her spirit cabinet on a road show, waiting for her cue, when I popped in her noggin.

Scared the bejeezus out of her, I imagine. Told me later she'd screamed and jumped so hard the cabinet fell over — landing on the door and locking her in. Terrified the audience. Best performance they'd seen — once Z played it off with her acting.

"Who are you?" she'd asked after, the connection still buzzingly live.

"I'm not too sure anymore," I lied. "Just call me a friend."

"Well *friend*," she doubted out loud, "tell me about it."

"About what?"

"It, it," she reiterated, "death, the end, the after. The great beyond. What do you see?"

"Well, it's not so great, for starters," I lit in. "Ain't no one here except this crazy codger waiting for what he won't say, and there's grass. Just grass," I said. "Boring, useless, sterile grass." At least where I was at. "Pointless lawn, better off digging it up for a garden," I anachronized. Deirdre would get it, eventually.

Misha's portal had led into the wildflower fields and fragrant forests where I was not allowed. No living may trespass or something like that, so I had to wait by the rivers. Old codger had said — wouldn't even take my coin for a ride. Said he wasn't the guy for that, but I had my doubts. Who else would be waiting beyond death's door?

"How disappointing," she soured.

"You're telling me," I sighed. It'd been a dead end — Dena nowhere to be found. I learned a few other things, though. "No one gets it right," I told Zestra.

"This does not surprise me," she shook her head. Strangely, though we'd been separated by veils and time and a few dimensions, I could still see her in my mind — every action she took, every gesture she made. I could view lots of people like that — ones I knew well anyway. Just close my eyes and go — no aphantasia there — but I couldn't act. Rather, they couldn't receive. Zestra and I could pass notes, though.

"What brings you back?" Zestra asked me here and now. "Surely your boring paradise was not so unpleasant as this." Her hand waved out to the grime and grit of the city. Perpetual darkness, even on a sunshone day. Sure, for some, it had nothing on the fields, but for me...

"All the times I lived," I smiled, "this is my favorite era." An era of pizazz and panache characterized by an emboldened spirit defiant of all that would bring it down. Plus, there were cool hats.

I wished I looked good in a hat. I just could never pull them off — never sat right on my head, I felt, no matter the face I took. But these people sure could. Smart suits and hats, glitzy dresses, and fascinating chapeaux. Peacock feathers everywhere.

The most beautiful part was no one's face was stuck in their phone. These people were present most of the moments of their life — way fewer Hylics hollowed out among them. Funny how almost losing everything will make you burn brighter.

"You come back to wear that ridiculous hat?" See? I told you. Zestra came around the table, pulling the curtain closed. Standing next to me, she hopped on tippy-toes to take the hat. "Too small for your head and your ears do strange things under it."

She stood back to get a better look, no longer backlit by the tent's entrance. Sights danced in her emerald eyes — reflections of all to come — as they flickered across my face.

"Much better," she smiled.

I wasn't sure what sort of smile it was. You can never tell with a seer and others of mysterious ways. Smiles could be very, very bad. Mine were, some of the time.

"You are like President's bear," she said, very close to me. This life, I was larger than — Zestra only came up to my chest — and a bit pudgy. "I pictured you different," she said, leaning in for a hug and kiss on the cheek.

The affection surprised me, to be honest. I hadn't felt the warmth of another in... a very, very long time. Since even before I'd darkened death's door. Cold and empty as I was after Dena — I still didn't feel I deserved it.

"So tense," she chided, stepping back to arm's length, her hands gripping my elbows. "Good to see you, friend." Her eyes drank me in.

"President's bear?" I laughed.

"Yes, Theodore's. Over in America," she poked my belly. "Cute and fluffy, like you."

"Oh, a Teddy Bear," I said, pulling away. "You know, it's bad luck to give a nameless stuffed bear? That's why they're all named Teddy now." Too close.

"Oh," she smiled, pinning me with her emerald gaze, "and what is your name, my President's bear?" She kissed me, pulling me down and stretching high herself — a touch of blackberries on her lips.

Whoa now. I tried to stop, but I melted into her. It had been a *long* time, and she wasn't taking no for an answer, regardless.

I lost myself for a while, feeling miserable and wrong after. The first of many such punishments.

I know you'd tell me this isn't safe, I texted. *But fuck that, I'm coming for you, Felix.* I was beyond tired of *safe,* of being trapped here — I grew legs for a reason.

I sent it into the etheric unread pile decorating Felix's lock screen. I hope he appreciated all my effort to keep him up to date.

I sat in silence, watching everyone about their business. I was packed and ready — like always — my shadow hanging from Maya-me as it pretended to do what she said. Hank drank as Evette poured, and I wondered just what he'd been like in his prime — before the world bent and bowed him. And that fiddle...

If you find yourself in the company of legends, you might just be one yourself. Sounds like a redneck joke, but looking around the room, I kind of felt it. I've never claimed to be normal, honest, but I never really considered myself mythical. I mean, I exist — mucosal membranes and everything — and I felt at home with this rag-tag bunch from a veritable storybook.

I mean...an immortal alchemist, a devil I know, somewhat of a ghost bestie, an eldritch moose, shapeshifters and seers, and a bloody-fingered murder-hobo itching to scritch. We were missing the gnomes — they were out hunting — and Tony — he had a project to finish.

"When do we begin?" Bill split a bone-toothed grin. "The moon aligns auspiciously for a darkened departure." I'd about had it with the way he talked. It hurt my brain to hear aloud — the dissonance alone schizzed my cerebrum. Half horny goat, half man, all unkempt with biological warfare for breath. Yet he spoke with the silvered tongue most would hardly shake a spear at — at least in writing. Aloud, it left much to be desired.

"Bill," I addressed the Bloodybell politely, "We need to establish some ground rules if you're coming with." *Like maybe bathing or brushing your teeth,* I really wanted to add.

His face soured in a flash.

"Our deal has been struck and sealed," he spoke the words of yore, "and you," he began to rage, "you would dishonor your given pledge?"

"Whoah, chill," I held my hands up. "I'm not dishonoring any deals, Bill," I said, using his name again in acknowledgment. "This is just so we all get along without the stabby-stabby."

"I have sworn my oath, no harm shall flow to you from me," he said, upstanding, bladed hands over his chest. I imagined if they did cross a heart, there'd be no need to hope for death, it'd be assured.

"And that takes care of rule number one: No killing — me, or StG, or anyone without my say." Had to minimize collateral damage.

"You promised me the charlatan thief's heart!" He slammed his fist down on the bar, sparks flying where his claws met the brass rail. Touchy much? He went on. "Carved out by my own hand!" He spread his fingers wide, relishing in the future murder.

"I promised you a chance at it," I said, cutting him off before he could go full Chad. "Against my better judgment, I might add." St Germain and Hank had assured me after that the Bloodybell couldn't even touch Felix, much less kill him, but it still gnawed at me. "You can certainly try, but without me, you'll never even find him."

"Number one," he gritted, "you've said. What be number two?"

"Two," I looked him square in the eye, "cut the arcane, tl;dr from here on out."

His mouth worked in silence, as if shaping a new tongue right then and there. Before he could use it, the building shook with a rafter-rattling rumble.

"Oh no," Maya-me began, suddenly holding bagpipes for some reason. "Just no," she whined.

The bottles behind the bar clanked together as they jittered, and everyone froze, bracing for some new attack. I smiled.

"Our ride's here!"

The salt spray made me sick. I don't like boats. Crossing the Channel was bad enough, and now I was stuck out in the middle of the Atlantic on a steel contraption that had no business being above the water — science and buoyancy be damned. And while we're at it, fuck you, Bernoulli. You and your flying metal death tubes — obsequious asshole. I'll take a goat if I want to fly, thank you very much.

"Looking rather green today, dear boy," St Germain ribbed me. The jostling upset my already turvy lunch, but I refrained from losing it.

"You're on the list now," I glared at the chipper asshole — bright as his diamond earring.

"What list?"

"You and Bernoulli,"

"What'd *I* do?" Wide-eyed confusion crinkled his face. "Him, I understand. Quite a piece of work, but moi?" The Count held his hand to his wounded chest, feigning hurt.

"You know what you did," I mock-glared at him. His response was genuine, though slight. I swear I saw a flash of true guilt before he played along.

"I confess," he announced for the world to hear. "I ate the last shrimp. It was delicious. I regret nothing." He huffed and turned heel back to the cabin. "Nothing!"

I followed, the fresh air having done me no good. I simply tried to put the boat and the rocking from my mind. Bad enough I felt the world spin on as it rounded the sun. *Frame of reference. Frame of reference.* I repeated the notion to myself, anchoring to a cosmic constant greater than the boat.

This was my first trip across the pond — preferring my own with the tree stone statue head — but not my alchemist friend's. He'd gallivanted about the colonies, gone west when west was all there was, and somehow circled back around.

"How'd you do it?"

"Full of sudden questions today, I see. Random ones, to boot." He flopped dramatically to the settee of our steamer room. "Pour me a brandy, will you? And while you're at it, enlighten me as to what you are referring."

"Cross the Pacific before there were big steamers like this," I clarified, pouring the brandy. He'd done it without hitching a ride from any explorers I knew.

"Simple," he said. "I walked." This time, I'm not sparing you the loquacious details — the answer that succinct. His lack of elaboration raised my suspicion. Highly uncharacteristic of the immortal, who seemed to think everyone had as long as he to listen.

"On water?" I quirked a brow. He confirmed my suspicion when he began fidgeting with his ear stud.

"The frozen kind, dear boy." He was lying straight to my face — albeit in an amusing way. If he didn't want to share, I wouldn't press.

"Speaking of ice," I dropped the subject, taking on another. "What's with the diamond?" I rarely saw him without the stud for decades now.

"Oh, it's an old superstition I picked up from a fellow traveling the world a while back," he waxed, more like himself. "Always wear one just valuable enough to buy a coffin and decent burial wherever you may go."

"What a strange notion for an immortal," I laughed.

"My turn," he detoured, "why the sudden urge to see the New World? Last time I asked, you looked as if I'd grown a third head."

That was one of those things I still hadn't figured out — fast travel — and so I tended to not. But now I had a need. Zestra had put me on to a legit psychic living in New York. Strange setup, there. Lots of naps.

"Got a lead." I leaned back with my brandy. "Need to follow it."

"Indeed?" St Germain was well aware of my quest for Dena's killer and helped when I let him. One of the few left I could count friend. Me, then, had pushed everyone away in grief, and most allowed it — or just died out. I found it hard to operate like that, so I was grateful for the company — even if I didn't elaborate.

"Gonna see what he says about this." I pulled out a small volume from my coat pocket. Bound in black with gilt lettering spelling out *The Black Pullet.* The book had come in vogue while I was out of town, written by the French chicken I'd met at a garden party a century ago.

This printing was in English, though, done a little later, with a *delightful* illustration of a man-headed chicken shitting out golden eggs — as depicted by the rays of sunshine beaming from their shells.

"Hack," St Germain derided, dismissing the Pullet. "Nothing substantive. Met that particular bird — who, might I add, doesn't even know the language of birds! — in the court of…" Yes, yes, we know you were a favorite of Louis Fifteen and got in pissing matches with Casanova over lavish dinners. See? I boiled down a fifteen-minute diatribe into a sentence. You're welcome.

"Not so sure, my friend." I politely waited until he was finished. "The chicken apparently had a rough trip to Egypt with Bonaparte and learned a few things from Tris under the Sphinx…"

"No shit," he sat back and thought. "Well," the quiet moment passed, "*I'm* off to find El Dorado or one of the other cities of Cibola," he started.

"Don't you have enough gold for lifetimes?" And could make as much as he needed. What'd he need with fountains of gold?

"Several," he waved his hand in dismissal, "but that's not the reason."

Before I could suss more out, my cosmic constant came untethered, and a roiling wave of nausea caught up to me. I may not be able to fast travel, but I sure as hell could skip this part.

Taking the fool key I felt away in my hand, I twisted, speeding the clock hands.

"Youseedearboythreedaysfromtheeltovarcrystalcany-fgerblad-re..." St Germain raced ahead.

"What is he..." one began.

"How?" the second simultaneous. Neither finished.

"Stop him!' third commanded.

"I do not control the remember!" one and two turned.

"He's come unstuck," the watching keeper spoke.

They awed, awaiting.

They are so going to be surprised when they see this, I gleamed. *You're not the only one who can pull shit, Felix!* Maybe he'd be proud of me. I was just trying to do what Felix would have done. Put the unflappable face on and stare into the abyss until it blinked, and I laughed in its ugly mug.

"Jya jyan," I weebed, giving my best Vanna White. "Secret tunnel!"

I'd led everyone back to the Gents' to show them my brilliant idea — a bit of an upgrade after Tony got hungry. It started out as me making a doggy door so Tony could go see Mama, but it'd be coming in surprisingly handy.

"Secret tunnel," I repeated to their blank stares. "No one? Okay, you're supposed to say 'through the...'" More blank stares. "Nevermind." Felix would have got it, I pouted inside.

"It's a lovely hole in the floor," St Germain peered into the depths. "Where the toilet was," he looked up at me. "Where's the toilet gone?"

"Tony ate it," I dismissed the complaint. "Bored the hole out for us, too."

"Symmetrical," Hank approved of the roundness.

"Us?" St Germain's eyebrows rose. "Dear girl, what on earth are you plotting?"

Everyone crowded around the tiny stall, trying to peek in — except for Elder, thank goodness. It was getting tight — too tight as I was pressed up against the cold tile. I thought better of my reveal and shooed them back out.

"Okay, so," I said when I could breathe again. "Secret tunnel..."

"You said that," Hank helped.

"Tony got in here by following the plumbing and chewing through the floor," I explained my irrationale. "So we can leave the same way."

"Long way to walk," Hank humphed, swaying one treacherous knee.

"Good thing you aren't going," I shot back, giving him an eye — somewhere between stink and dare. "It is. That's why I asked Tony to call his Mama to come pick him — and hopefully us — up."

Maya-me blew a FWAH on the still-present pipes — for reasons known only to her — and stormed off. My shadow shook its head and tailed slightly behind.

Tony poked his fuzzy head out of the bathroom, confusion in his eyes as he sought the sound and saw me, then another me. And it was just all confuzzle from him.

"Oh, Tony," I cooed, "I'm right here, baby." I bent down so he could run up my arm and around my shoulders, swaying as he shifted and settled — he was no longer a small long-boi. "You've got a little schmutz." I wiped the corner of his beak where he'd been eating whatever.

"Back to the tunnel," St Germain interjected.

"Secret tunnel," I amended, gathering together the rest of my pack. "Get your shit together."

"Dear girl, my shit is *always* together." The alchemist seemed unconcerned about the belongings in his room; rather, he just checked his pockets for items within. I liked to travel light myself, but his easy air about it was impressive. "And yes, the *secret* tunnel," he went on. "Where does it lead?"

"Out," I oversimplified. That was all that mattered, really. "It leads out. Secretly, so we can pull off this ruse," I said. "Can't exactly just waltz out the front door and expect them to buy Maya is me. You and Bill? Sure, maybe, but not me."

The murder-hobo had donned his bloody cloak — freshly soaked, it seemed. I refrained from asking 'in what' — and kicked his hooves against the floor as if they itched. Eager to be on our way.

"A fair point," St Germain allowed, considering. "And then?"

"Once we're away from prying eyes, Bill can *walk* us where we need," I smiled. "Right Bill?"

"He can?" The alchemist's eyebrows rose as the Bloodybell's creased in a frown.

Didn't think I knew that, I thought as I smiled a bit smug, *did you?*

"Thanks, Trudy," I said, doffing my cap like a proper gentleman. Ridiculous or not, I still like the hats, damnit. "Ed! How are you?" I crossed the room to shake his hand. "Look like you could use a nap," I laughed.

"Edgar, please," he corrected for the thousandth time — all proper with his slicked-back hair and starched collar. I'd given up on name tags — they *were* coming in vogue, but I just started calling people what I would.

"Sure, Edgar," I amended, not wanting him to throw me out on my keister. Play nice, I reminded myself. Back to the point. "I find myself in need of somnistic answers yet again," I said, holding out the book of my enemy.

"Again?" Edgar eyed the book dubiously. "Every time I delve there, I feel sick," he frowned. "Nothing good can come from those forsaken pages."

"There, you're right, Mr. Cayce," I said. "And yet I still humbly seek," I said, pulling an envelope stuffed with cash from my suit pocket, "a donation for your institute."

Edgar eyed the envelope as his wife came in with refreshments on a tray, along with a pad and pencil. She startled upon seeing the sum, looking to her husband with a slightly urgent nod. Seemed they were in need of the cash.

At the nod, he relented with a suffering sigh, accepting the cash along with the black leather tome. The man was a devout Christian and felt his abilities a gift from God — discounting most of his prophecies and metaphysical insights as blasphemous mumbo-jumbo if he could not reconcile them with his faith. He disliked taking money directly for readings, refused for the most part, but he was less strict with *donations*.

"What shall I seek?" The man known as the Sleeping Prophet slipped his shoes off and sat on his couch, laying back for a nap — the book tucked under his head.

"Just whatever you can tell me about the writer." I was still tracking the Pullet down. "Any clues would be helpful." The book was two hundred years old by that point and the trail had long grown cold. But he didn't know that part.

Question in mind, he shut his eyes. His breathing quieted as he relaxed into trance.

"Well butter my butt and call me a biscuit," Eddie said with a gruffer voice, sitting upright and cracking his neck. "If it ain't the bornless come again," he eyed me. "Toots, gimme a cigar and a snort." This he directed at Trudy.

That's the funny thing about the mercurial edge — the border of sleep and wake that gives rise to the dream — anything can come through, connect. Especially one's repressed self like Eddie here. The dichotomy was amusing, I thought.

"Glad you're here, Eddie." I leaned forward as Trudy brought him a bourbon and a cigar, leaving us alone after. No wonder Edgar felt sick after my visits — it wasn't *just* the vile nature of the Pullet's tome, though I suspected Eddie needed the drink to steel himself. "Think you can help my chicken hunt?"

"Sure sure," he drank. "Just a minute." Lighting the cigar, he took a few puffs. "Why you keep poking at it is beyond me," he said. "But," he shrugged, "your money."

"You don't know what they did," I darkened at the subtle dismissal. How anyone could *move on* as he suggested was unfathomable.

"Yeah," he locked eyes with me, "I do, old man." He took another drink. "Saw it right here," he tapped his temple. "Horrific, *I know*."

I frowned. He drank.

"And I'm sorry for your loss, but what're you gonna do about it?" Compassionate eyes looked to mine for their answer, finding nothing. "You can't bring her back," he said, "I know you've tried." He sat back, draining his bourbon and staring into the glass bottom. "Never heal, you keep pickin' at it like this," he said seriously.

"Anything new in the Records?" Eddie, on instinct alone, had drunk from the Mnemosyne — sister to Lethe — when he'd nearly died aged seven. Gave him access to knowledge and memory I didn't even have. Handy, that.

"West and west again. There, by the river red, above reflects below," he recited. "The ritual begun by the repellant man come into its rich fullness."

Repellant, repulsive, same diff, I bit back.

"And I see…" He flinched, eyes rolling about. "I see a heart, beating still, circled by a nest of serpents."

My blood ran chill. The Order had picked up where the Mage's cabal left off — they intended to descend an Angel.

Well.

Shit.

"You first." I frantically motioned Bill ahead toward the hole. "Hurry!"

They had come again. Oil-slicked creatures pouring through the broken window. Had they known what we planned? I could see the melee through the door as St Germain closed it tight.

The gnomes had returned, thank goodness, and knocked the bumps about while Garth covered Hank and a newcomer seeking refuge the fjøsnisser had found. The giant bouncer layed about with his good arm making the goo go splat. Evette even got a hit in with a hefty bourbon bottle, cracking a bumper's skull, as she stood next to Maya-me staying to the outskirts of the fight. My shadow wrestled with an overly large attacker as Elder snorted and stomped, hooves tearing into the inky mess.

My stomach turned — I felt like I was abandoning them to hopeless peril. I knew they could handle themselves, and we needed to be gone, but it still felt like I was turning my back on my friends.

"Never turn your back on a Bloodybell and never get too far away, else they'll step out of sight and likely betray." Felix's words stuck from his quickie crash course — somehow guessing I'd have to deal with the likes of Bill o'deSoul again.

"Come on, hurry!" I shoved the Bloodybell roughly forward as his eyes hungered for the violence beyond the door. The words had made no sense at the time, but I was slowly putting things together. "Careful of the last step, don't land in the squelch."

"Squelch?" His tendency toward arcane speech denied, the murder-hobo had become rather mono-syllabic — as if he had to chew his multitude of words down before speaking, grimacing as if pained all the while.

"The bottom isn't exactly solid," I said, "more non-Newtonian." I stepped to the first rung, glancing back toward the door as I hovered over the abyss below.

"Still a hack," St Germain muttered at the name. Always a dropper, our immortal. "Squelch is as good a name as any to deny him undue credit. They'll be alright," St Germain reassured me, catching my hesitation. "Hank has yet to play."

It still galled at me as I began to descend. Tony clung to the tunnel wall at my side, keeping pace with me. St Germain came last, one lingering look as he lit the new lantern, sending it down behind me.

Blue flame lit the darkness, clearly delineating the confined space.

"You couldn't have made it any bigger, Tony?" His fur ruffled up against my face, barely squeezing through beside me. He squealed like an ungreased wheel bearing, threatening to crack. "I know, I know," I sighed. "I'm sorry. You did a wonderful job for the short amount of time you had."

"How much further, dear girl," St Germain called from above.

"Not far, just a dozen more yards, Bill…" I looked down to see how close to the bottom he was.

SPLAT-SLURP the Squelch sucked at him. Too close, judging from that sound.

The one that followed curdled my brain — a pitched anguish scream gut-punched its way up the shaft as the Bloodybell stabbed down into the muck with wicked malice. The noise devolved into guttural squeals that may have been the goat-thing cursing. Slowly he sank as he lashed about. Such is the danger of quicksand.

The scene was oddly reminiscent of our first encounter — except this time, he wasn't faking the distress.

"Quit struggling!" I slid down the ladder rail, stopping just short of the slurp before jumping to the side tunnel. "You'll just sink faster." And I needed him alive yet.

Grabbing a steel scaffolding pipe, I ran it out for Bill, clumsily banging it off the non-Newtonian surface into which he sank — rang rather like a bell, surprisingly. I never expected such a clarion sound from a pipe-smacking squelchy muck.

"Take it!" I urged the murder-hobo to grab hold so he could pull himself out.

I'm not sure which gulped and groaned more — Bill or the slurping muck. This trip was so full of super not-pleasant sounds I *never* wanted to hear again, and we'd barely just begun.

"I thought I said *not* to stand on the squelch?" Once freed, I checked the murder-hobo over in the light of the floating lantern, heeling my every step.

"I abided the instruction," Bill said, flinging brown sludge from his finger-needles. I really did *not* need to know what made up the muck. "That creature *attacked* me," he claimed, stabbing sharply toward it.

My eyes shot toward the smooth surface of the squelch, seeing no signs of an attacker. Even Bill's divots had begun filling in like a slurry of wet cement.

"There's nothing there," I said.

"In darkness there was," Bill insisted.

"Well," I turned toward the muck, "If there is, I'll invoice it for back rent. StG?" I poked my head out to look up the ladder. "You coming or what?"

"Here, dear girl," he puffed. "Greatness cannot be rushed. It arrives in the due course of time." His words meandered on despite his seeming lack of breath. "Have you extricated our compatriot from his predicament?"

"How is it you allow him the words you deny me?" Bill made a reasonable complaint. It was entirely unfair to the murder-hobo — but life's not fair.

"Him, I can tune out," I pointed. "No offense." St Germain waved off the remark. "You? Your breath stinks of rotted cabbage and raw sewage, and I'd rather not be synesthetically assaulted like that every time you open your foul mouth." His words toxic at every level and in every sense.

Rage filled his eyes at the insult I'd levied, but I just didn't care anymore. He could damn well get over his fragile sensibilities. Before he could even move, Tony coiled around his stubby arms and goat legs, binding his murderous instruments to his side. He threw his head wildly around, trying to catch Tony with his hooked horns.

"I said no killing," I snapped as Tony shoved his porcelain-rending beak in the murder-hobo's face. "If your ego is going to be a problem, say so, and I'll end this farce now."

Furious eyes fixed on mine — I didn't blink. Instead, his goat-slit eyes turned down and to the side, the tension coiled in his limbs melted away.

"Wonderful," I said, turning to St Germain. "Let's go shopping for books."

I smiled and skipped down the tunnel where Tony's Mama waited to give us a ride.

"I'm heading West," I said. The subway rumbled under my feet as I stepped out onto Shaw, hat in hand. "Need you to look after things for a bit, Olya."

No name tag, but none was needed. Her name I finally knew. About five feet and one half inch tall, she skipped beside me as we walked down the street.

"What's West?" Her silvery curls bounced as she skipped, flailing out as her head turned to me.

"That way," I pointed with my hat, smiling. "Where you come back from when you go too far East," I crossed my arms the other direction.

"Like this?" She appeared of a sudden right behind me, leaning into view.

"Something like that," I smirked at the pixie girl. She'd been a good student, surpassing myself in some of the tricks and cons. Certainly more personable, in that ADHD kinda way. "Look," I said seriously, "I'm going to be gone a long while."

"On purpose?" She feigned hurt.

"You'll be fine," I assured her. "The Saffron School for Confidence is in good hands, I'm certain," I said, handing her a key. "Keep it safe."

"Aye aye," she fake saluted. Over-drama suited her spiciness. "Are you coming back?"

"Someday," I felt, "yes." I knew then, as I know now, it was going to be a long trip with a long wait at the end — not that time truly mattered at the school or for me.

Dubious. Her face screamed it with nary a word as if she knew this was goodbye.

"Oh!" I almost forgot. "From now on, say your name is Helena," I said, resting my hat on my head.

Only-time-I'll-call-her-Helena stopped short, shorter than she already was, tasting the name on her tongue. Her face puckered as if it were a lemon.

"Why Helena?" The struggle was real; it weighed heavy on her tongue even as she said it. But that was the point, wasn't it?

"Reasons," I said, waving fare-the-well behind me.

Secrets of the Trees

I DON'T THINK I'M a nice person. Strange thing to say, I know, but I feel confident in that assessment after flipping off the little old lady behind the wheel of a land boat as I zipped by in the T-bird.

In my former self's defense, he did not know she was a lady, nor old, nor little — though one could reasonably assume those things by the slow weaving and constant braking, except the lady part — until seeing her in the rearview.

I'll never forget the face she made. A mix between shock, confusion, a dash of anger, but mostly sadness. Except, maybe I would. Forget, I mean.

I already had once — at least — before.

I don't know where she was going, where she'd been, or why she was crying, but she was in the way. And apparently I was impatient...

Odd quality for an immortal. You'd think that would be the first thing they teach you at immortal school, but I haven't relived that part of my life — or lives — yet.

I was somewhat in the driver's seat now — at least from what I saw — but not totally. Past-me still held sway, and unless I really focused on it, I just did the same things over and over again.

Where was I? Oh, not nice. Right.

I went back even further, gripping the fool's key away in my hand as I wound other hands backward, finding myself relieving a pair of bootleggers of their stash.

Well...at least I *asked* them politely.

"Now, if you'd be so kind as to hop on out before you grow some extra holes," I said, the fool's key turning into a gun in my grip, one that I shoved in the driver's ear, "I'd be appreciative." See? Polite. Even when I was soaked to the bone in the drencher I found myself in.

Shotgun went for his sawed-off as Sassy shoved a full barrel under the guard's nose — a Sassy-pants-special with the trigger guard filed off. There weren't exactly many guns made to fit his big hands, so we improvised. It looked ridiculously tiny — the entire stock fit in his grip.

"Over here, sweetheart," Sassy cooed the muscle, turning his head with the barrel. "I'd hate to ruin that pretty face, but hun, this thing's loaded with slugs aching for a kiss," the Bigfoot smooched.

We'd stopped them easily enough. The flood Lenny's storm caused detoured the truck off the open flats to higher ground where Sassy shoved a tree across the road. They stopped and I hopped on up to the running board, asking right politely — as I said — and so here we are.

I bounced and trundled the truck through the muck we'd made after Sassy'd cleared the road. Lenny sat up in another tree and screeched at the pair, cracking bolts from his eyes as they leveled threats like:

"Do you know who we work for?" And "You're dead!" Among such chestnuts as "When we get loose...", "You'll be sleeping with..." and other entirely ineffectual provocations.

I did them the courtesy, at least, of looking mildly concerned with my fake face. They'd had a rough day, and what did I care? It was just another mask.

Not often do bootlegger henchmen get held up at slug-point by a giant ape-man, a literal thunderbird sparking lightning, and…well…an entirely unremarkable guy — especially next to those two. They were going to have quite the story to tell, if anyone believed them.

Though, if their boss was who I thought, he just might. And that's exactly what I wanted. My fake face grimaced, remembering. I shook it off before it could stick — the face and the memory. Couldn't be pulled astray; I still had things to do here.

The truck lurched to the side, nearly tipping as Sassy landed on the running board. "Where you goin', sweetie? You missed the turn."

I looked around, bewildered as I braked, the rain had come on harder and the dim headlights only reached so far.

"You sure?"

If you've ever wondered why I call him Sassy-pants, the look he just gave me through the window should remove all doubt. Lips pursed, eyes drawn tight, head cocked back in the perfection of *Mhmmm.*

"I think I know where my own hideout is, sugar." Always with the sweets talk. Sassy liked his beer, but I've never seen him turn down a sugar-laden cocktail, either. Damian's probably figured that out by now, but I wasn't going to volunteer it in case of future bets. Lenny had been mad about that one.

Wow, just wow, Lenny had complained as Molly drove us to the lakeside camp. *Did I say you could bet me?* Only I could hear him, and, with my hangover, wished I couldn't.

It's a lock, I tried to placate. *You know how Sassy drinks. We just have…*

No, Lenny interrupted to finish. *I did not.* He was in a huff, racing along faster than Molly was actually driving.

"Easy there, speed racer," I teased her as she looked all sorts of confused.

"I'm not doing *anything*," she complained, wide-eyed. "Your car's got a mind of its own!"

"You don't know the half of it," I laughed, shutting my eyes against the aching sun. *Go easy on the kid, Lenny,* I thought at him.

The engine rumbled a complaint in response.

"Is it running out of gas?" She opened her hands a little, looking for a better view of the gages. It didn't really matter. Lenny was driving, not Molly. I mean, what sort of Xennial — or whatever — knows how to drive a stick? She'd just hopped in and we went. I guess he liked her. All my friends seemed to.

"Start looking for one of your requisite sketchy gas stations, just in case." I didn't say he's just being a crankcase. "We need some bait if…"

"Yooohooo," Sassy waved. Damnit, I'd drifted. We'd got where we were going, and I hadn't a clue how.

The hidden glen Sassy called home was breathtakingly beautiful. The mountain path was obscure, to say the least, having to go through at least one cave to the back side of a sheer cliff. No wonder he was the world hide-and-seek champ.

Bright and sunshiny, Lenny's temper didn't reach here where Sassy held sway and, from the looks of the switchback trail, the truck wouldn't reach there either — 'there' being Sassy's house by the fishing pond, nestled cozy in the valley.

Cedar shake and slate, tin sprouting at odd angles — a charming mix of hand-crafted and store-bought, or -stole as the case may be. Almost all of it varying levels of porch. I'd once heard it described as a redneck pagoda by a blind rabbit.

A veritable Shangri-La shared only with a select few.

I popped out of the truck and took a closer look at the crumbling edges of the switchback and the boulder-studded drop below. Four-wheel drive only gets you so far, then you need a vehicle with other talents.

Lacking such talents, my foot slipped.

"Woah there, big fella," Sassy snatched me by the collar — my tattered hat, unfortunately, fluttered to the boulders below. Gone, I'd have removed it out of respect, but I could no longer — a single tear at the honor denied. My hat deserved better.

"Shame," Sassy went on, hauling me to the back of the truck, where he began unloading the bootlegger's haul. He'd been after the alcohol; I was in it for something different.

"You never liked my hat," I accused, slightly distracted. No one had. What was wrong with them? "Should have saved it," I dusted my britches, "I'd have been fine." I rummaged through the goods. "Where is it…"

"I'll remember that next time you're in dire peril, sweet cheeks," he harrumphed. "Grab a crate," he grabbed two, chock full of booze, "we're hoofing it from here."

I took a last look around, finding no gold.

Where is he?

"Dear girl," St Germain never said my name. Was that a peculiarity of immortals? What? They meet so many they can't keep our names straight? My fingers clutched tighter.

"M - O - L - L - Y," I spelled it out for him. Loud over the rumble. "Mah-lee, you should try it sometime."

"Why, dear girl, I invented the dreadful stuff," he sniffed, derailed from his line of inquiry. "Named it after this delightful young…" He saw me glazing over. "Nevermind. Just another one of my misused wonders. Feel like I'm on it now, though," he ducked a stalactite, burying his face in Long-Mama's back-fur as she serpentined her way through the tunnel. "Whoah!"

You know, the secret one.

"No, whoah, only go!" I laughed. "Go, go, go!"

"Go where?" St Germain managed to finally ask.

"Always start looking the last place you saw it," I said. "Not counting the bar, that was a bookstore."

St Germain raised an eyebrow. "Which bookstore?"

"Lenore's," I smiled, remembering the cavern of books. Marty'd hoarded a lot of them over the years. I wasn't quite sure how he made money, none of the books ever seemed to move, but Lenore's remained open nonetheless. "It's this great hole-in-the-wall kinda place Felix showed me, and there's a back room where…"

"I hate to break the tour itinerary up," Bill interrupted, "but methinks we're being followed."

"What!?" I snapped my head around. The whole point of the secret tunnel plan was that it *was* secret! I peered deeper into the dark, the lantern light I held close, ruining my sight beyond. "I don't see anything."

Tony made a distressed grinding sound — like a fork caught in a disposal — feeling my agitation. Long-mama fwanked in response, soothing her kit with her murmurs. I think at one point she ate a train and the horn got lodged in her throat.

"There it be, though you do not see," he rhymed. I shot him a warning glance against his slipping tongue. "See the shadow slick and ripple?"

"He's not wrong," St Germain pitched in his two cents. "The liminal flow of light *is* distorting ever so…"

"Is there something, or not?" I cut him off while thinking: *Why must I suffer the terminally loquacious?*

My question answered itself when long-mama lurched to one side, rolling as the tunnel collapsed in our wake. Well shit, so much for *secret tunnel*. No going back now.

I clung tight to the white fur, burying myself deep as I tried not to get scraped off on the rugged rock walls of the tunnel while long-mama regained her bearing.

"What's happening?" I screamed into the muffling fluff, unable to see anything, only hope and wait for the ride to stop.

Noises… Loud and banging and screaming fought their way to my ears as we jolted. I heard St Germain shouting what sounded like Latin sprinkled with epithets of many languages and felt the flashes of light that followed, so bright they tore through my eyelids or maybe through the back of my skull to the front of my face.

Tony wrapped around my shoulders, holding me closer to his mama, taking the brunt of the scuff as we ground along. Long-mama roared like steel beams ripping in her anger. How dare *any* attack her young in her own tunnels!

Somewhere along the way, my brain had enough and just noped out. Not the best survival instinct, for sure, but maybe a little of Felix's luck rubbed off on me.

The orange-striped face that butted my head awake looked perpetually curious with the classic tabby M on his forehead. He *mrowed* a good morning at me.

"Well hello, Elliot," I scratched behind his ear. "Now, how'd I get here?" I asked as he purred, relishing the attention. I should probably have been dead.

"Sorry about that whole attention thing, Sassy," I drank. We'd been doing that a lot — currently outside at a bonfire near the porch. "Didn't really know what I was doing at the time." And I hadn't. Well, I sort of knew, but I didn't know just how *long* I'd have their attention. "Was mad about Dena and them not giving a shit."

"Oh honey, you can *always* have my attention," he fluttered his eyelashes over his keg. "And it's true, they don't give a shit — too preoccupied with their games and their pedantic rules. Can't stand those pricks."

"So why were you partying with them?" I didn't really know him yet, but later learned just how much of a solitary creature he was. He partied hard, but that wasn't his scene.

"Erl begged me to go," Sassy rolled his eyes. "Wanted to show me off to his friends like I was some sort of trophy." He flipped what I've come to know as his Farrah hair at that. He really *was* something else.

"Can you really blame him?" Like I said, I was drunk. Might as well play along.

Sassy eyed me, considering. "No," he cocked his head back. "I *am* a fabulous catch, but he done fucked up," Sassy sniffed derisively. "I dumped his ass after he showed out like that."

I raised my glass in salute.

"Wise," I said. "You don't need anyone who can't keep their liquor."

"Ain't that the truth, honey," he laughed and drank some more. Bootleggers' stock was already running low — we'd need to pull another job soon to replenish. Sassy got thirsty. "You keep up just fine," he cooed.

"Flattered, but you know I'm faithful," I flashed my ring. It wasn't the first pass he'd made, and it was sweet, but we were drunk. He knew better.

"To a corpse," he let bitterness slip and my eyes must've darkened deathly. "I'm sorry," he quickly amended, realizing. "I shouldn't have said that…"

"No." Stone sober again. "You shouldn't."

"But you do need to forgive yourself," he went on, going there. "Move on with your long life," Sassy saddened, drawing from experience. We had similar problems — the dreadful loneliness all immortals and those nigh-to seem to share.

I sulked into my shine. It tasted of elderflower, tickling at a memory dulled.

"I know!" Sassy brightened again. "You should find yourself a nice tree and settle down," he giggled preemptive of his joke, "put down some roots."

"You're drunk," I couldn't help but laugh. "A tree?"

"I am," he agreed, "but that doesn't mean I'm wrong, sweetie. Trees are wonderful people."

"Okay, I'm drunk then," I was, slipping back into the buzz from the anger flash. "Because I have no clue what you're talking about."

"A nice, mature tree," he went on. "Should have about your life-span. What…two, three centuries?"

"Something like that," I didn't go into specifics.

"There you go! It's perfect. Done," he grinned. "I know someone perfect."

Some time after that — things tend to get blurry after drinking that much — I found myself trodding down a firefly path. The dusk had settled in, must have been three days later — it'd taken another day of drinking for Sassy to convince me and a day to sleep it off.

"There's wisdom in trees," he'd said. "Even if you and Hazel," — that was her name, apparently, or species? I wasn't too sure among trees — "don't hit it off, I think you'd still be good for each other. You need other friends than me and Lenny."

I objected to the notion. I had friends. Well, at one point I did.

Now, I wasn't too sure.

"Yoo-hoo," I heard a voice call. "Over here," the leaves rustled.

I could see no one talking. I wasn't exactly sure what to expect from a blind date with a tree — Sassy had declined any further details. Just told me to follow the fireflies until I met up with Hazel. Said I'd know.

Well I didn't, and for as much as I'd forgot, I didn't like not knowing.

"Hello?" I slowed and circled, trying to decide where I'd heard the voice.

"You're getting colder," she teased.

I turned, moving some leafy branches aside. Maybe she was hiding?

"Ow!" Before I could call out again, a nut had cracked me in the head. Hard.

"Aren't you the naughty one," she tittered. "Trying to get under my skirts on the first date." I felt the branch I held turn, holding my hand in hers.

"I'm sorry?" I was incredibly confused as I watched the tree shrink into the curves of a woman.

"Incorrigible," she playfully scoffed. "But what else should I expect from one of *his* friends?" Her laugh was rich and warm. Her eyes, now that she had them, danced with the light of the fireflies. Green hair, as Molly'd once had, flowed down her back as she gave me a wicked smile.

"Aren't you *one of his friends*, too?" I shot my own wicked grin back.

"Why," she slipped closer, "I do believe I am."

"Good, good, keep him distracted," one said, clutching hands.

"He's learning," another countered. "And gaining."

"Losing our grip," the third.

"Leave it to me," the last spoke.

We snuck out to Lenore's, I texted Felix one-handed by the flickering lantern light, *though our sneak wasn't too high.* I frowned, thinking back to the harried escape from the Last Chance. I listened for a buzz or a ding. He never kept his phone on silent. Nothing. Of course he wasn't here — that'd be too easy.

"Well good morning, dear girl," St Germain greeted me as I left the cozy napping nook with Elliot in arm, my safety lamp floating silently behind. "Tea?" He offered me a steaming mug of what smelled like Darjeeling.

"Got any Irish?" Lordy Lordy did I need it. "What happened?"

"Just some of Kentucky's finest," he passed me the
Woodford. Odd pairing, but these were strange times.
He made no effort to answer my question — that wasn't
ominous at all. Perhaps I needed the bourbon first, answers
later.

Elliot jumped down to demand tribute from the alchemist as
was his rightful due as lord protector of this establishment.
Those were the thoughts he fed my way, at least. He had a
high opinion of himself, certainly, but then he *was* a cat, after
all. Elliot shot me a glance at that — a rather haughty one
— and I gave him a smug look right back, which he dutifully
ignored as he made his wish for pets known with a mrow,
arching into St Germain's leg.

"Well hello," he reached down to pet the tabby cat who
turned at the motion as if to say *with your eyes* in an indignant
fashion before striding off, tail held high. "Nice cat," St
Germain laughed.

"Don't mind him," Marty said, coming into the room with
another book for the infinite shelves. "Molly!" He smiled,
seeing me upright and about. "Gave us a fright," he added,
pouring his own mug of bourbon with a splash of tea.

"Everything secure?" St Germain's eyebrow rose as he
asked. Was what secure? What was going on?

"The doors are shuttered and locked," Marty assured, "and
the lesser-known ways, too, are barred," he nodded. "Elliot's
gone to patrol." Marty sipped from his mug shaped like a
card catalog.

I felt sickness hold my stomach. They weren't telling me
something.

"So," I started, ignoring the questions I *didn't* want answers
to until the bourbon took hold. "Why are we fortifying
the bookstore?" I shifted my glance between Marty and St
Germain, waiting for either to answer.

"It seems, dear girl," St Germain began, "the Last Chance is not the only place under siege." The unflappable immortal's face darkened, jollies silenced for the moment as he sipped.

"Wherever Felix found himself," Marty added, "*they*'ve come looking."

"The ubiquitous *they* strike again," I sighed. "Any clue who?"

"The corrupt," Marty said after a look to the alchemist. "The innocent, caught up in someone's dirty laundry." The way he spoke volumetrically added to the cryptic qualities of this whole mess — casting much shade. St Germain shifted in his chair at that, but I didn't press. I avoided it and all the other questions screaming in the back of my brain.

I wanted to escape. I wanted to escape all this crap suddenly thrust upon me. Escape into a book, perhaps. *That would be nice,* I thought as I got up to silently peruse the shelves while the two men sat and doured at the situation we found ourselves in.

Marty'd tired of idle silence, it seemed, as he, too, rose, taking the tea tray with him. Hopefully to fetch more.

My finger trailed along spines — titles familiar and not — feeling the words within. Connecting to the pages. I inhaled their luscious scent deeply, smiling at the myriad scenes popping into my head. One benefit of being, well, me.

"I never get tired of that smell," I uttered, pulling a particularly well-loved tome from Marty's shelves.

"That's so metal," St Germain said of the blue. I quirked an eyebrow, confused by his commentary. "Am I using that right?"

"I don't follow," I kinda lied, my eyes feigning wide. I had a feeling I knew, but I was tired of his bush-beating and the bourbon was kicking in.

"*You* like the smell of rotting corpses," he stepped in it. "Tattooed ones at that!" I think he thought he was funny.

"And what's so metal about liking books?" I wasn't letting him out of it. "Lots of people like books, like their smell, like their texture," I gestured about the bookstore nook. "Marty here wouldn't have a shop full of those tattooed rotting corpses — as you put it — if they didn't."

"True," St Germain allowed, "but you're a tree!" His voice crescendoed at the exclaimed declaration. "Irony abounds! Obfirmatis Ilex, unless I miss my guess."

"Trenynn," I corrected, though he plowed right through it.

"I've read up on all the Obfirmatis clans," he went on. "Fascinating culture! Why I once heard about a..." I had to calm myself. Be nice. He doesn't know any better. "But I've never met an Obfirmatis in person!"

"We don't like that name," I snipped. "It's rather offensive, in fact." Like most names applied in blind ignorance.

"I had no idea." The alchemist rose, coming to look me in the eye. "My most sincere apologies, dear girl," he said, taking my hand. "Please, enlighten me." Genuine curiosity lit in eyes that had seen much over the centuries he'd apparently lived. He craved to know.

"That *taxonomy* was given my kind by pompous pricks who thought they knew everything under the sun and stars..."

"I can think of a few," he muttered, "Paracelsus..."

"Hush," I cut him off. "You asked, I'm answering."

St Germain reflexively opened his mouth to speak, before dramatically shutting it again — an act that seemed to require great effort.

"We call ourselves the Trenynn," I repeated, careful of my pronunciation.

"Tree-nen?" he tried, unable to stop speaking. "Isn't that a little on the nose?"

"Treh, treh," I corrected. "Short e. Your people said it wrong and shortened it."

Elliot tried to say it, too — popping back in from who knows where.

Actually, it was more like 'bleh, hrech, gleh' — in other words, retching up a hairball. Quite angrily, I must say, from the vibes I felt. Must be a rough one.

"Poor guy." I reached to ease him, sending sympathy and calm. Bad idea.

The pissed-off tabby hissed and yowled at me in return, eyes going wide as he snapped his head toward me. Something had him in a mood — more than the hairball. He paced as he hurked — tail twitching then frizzing.

Jingle-jangle, the door chime rang.

"I thought Marty locked u…" St Germain began as Elliot bolted, coughing up…smoke?

"The hell?" I shot after him, coming to the door in time to see the tabby cat leap and hurk a massive ball of…flames? My brain still wouldn't connect what I was seeing… toward the bookshop door.

The streaking fire-hair-ball-wad-whatever streaked across the room toward the very startled face of Bill o'deSoul.

Days passed in a spuddle, it seemed. Holding up bootleggers, crooks, thugs — any sort of ne'er-do-well that could be taking *his* coin for me to bite. A whole bunch of busy-nothing. Spuddle, indeed.

That's a word I'd like to bring back, I distracted myself, rummaging through a ruffian's pockets.

"What is?" Apparently out loud, as Sassy asked what I was on about.

"Didn't realize I was talking," I mumbled, grabbing for gold. "Spuddle, that's the word." The thug groaned, probably objecting in his dreams — or whatever it is you see when you're knocked out.

"Sounds kinky," Sassy quivered with feigned pleasure. "What is it?" Sassy grinned, fixed his hair and eyed the prone thug.

I sighed. I liked Sassy, but I was getting a little tired of the constant *in-your-end-o* as he incessantly entendred.

"Heard it when I was a kid," I said. "Means to be extremely busy," I said, biting the gold, "whilst achieving absolutely nothing," I grimaced, tossing it down on the poor sap's stomach. He didn't get paid enough for this as it was.

"Not one of his?" Sassy nudged the thug with his size twenty. Wide.

"Spuddle." Inside and out. Wheels turned as I thought of what to do next. We'd been getting nowhere in our hunt — well, my hunt, really.

Sassy was in it for the fun and booze. Lenny still joined in out of boredom, but not much anymore. It'd been months of successless spuddle.

Okay, tired of the word now. Instead, I drifted, sifting through the memories as I felt the key turn faster in my hand. Days passed like seconds as the stars and moon and sun wheeled above through blues and reds and blacks and one incredibly bright gold limned with green aurora.

I found myself again with Hazel, laying with her beneath the branches of her...well...

"How does it work again?" We'd gotten along well enough — not the fiery passion Sassy begged some tea be spilt about — but more companionship. We'd both lost loved ones we held dear and were trying to put the pieces of ourselves back together. It wasn't love, but it was comfortable.

And the sex was pretty good.

I wasn't going to tell Sassy that, though. I'd never hear the end of 'wood' jokes. For once, I didn't feel like I was punishing myself by being with her, and I didn't want to ruin it.

"Well, you see..." she demurred, eyes teasing me as her hand explored down low. "You have this branch that sticks out."

I rolled my eyes. Horny, the lot of them.

"With your kid watching?" I feigned a shocked face, scandalizing her. "Have you no shame, woman?" I laughed.

"Oh that." She looked up into the branches of the young hazel tree beneath which we lay. "That *is* a sprout from my seed, yes." She leaned in closer, kissing my neck. "But it will never be my child." She sighed. "It lacks the spark of necessary awareness."

"So, how do you have kids?" It wasn't sex; that was purely recreational for her.

"The Trenynn propagate through learning." Hazel's eyes went wistfully distant. A regret? A child lost? She'd never shared that part of her before or since. "We teach. We whisper to our saplings the tales of old. We spread the customs of our kind. And we wait."

"Wait for what?"

"Reason and understanding to grow," she said. "For their soul to no longer be empty."

"To see which won't be Hylic," I nodded, understanding blossoming. People were the same way. They may be *alive*, but they weren't all necessarily there.

"I don't care for the word," Hazel frowned. "But yes, close enough."

Oh, right. *Hylic* meant wooden to the Greeks. Bereft of animas. Empty. The Greeks didn't know a damn thing.

"Well, you're anything but," I smiled, running my fingers through her now auburn hair, having been visited by the ginger fairy recently. Soon it'd fall out and she'd be bald for the winter.

"Play for me?" She sighed and changed the subject.

Memory tickled and my hands went to a velvet bag. When had I gotten that? I couldn't recall, but somehow I did know how as my fingers felt their way around the wooden flute, gifted me by the Elder Mother — something inside told me that. Still more bubbles even as I relived these lives — and I began to play the familiar trills.

Hazel stilled and relaxed as she slept, shifting back into her tree form before my eyes. Rough bark slithered over her skin as she stretched higher for the sky — fingers feathering out to branches and twigs. Leaves, now red, quivered as I played beneath her branches, twining up above her sprouts.

With other eyes, I saw her blue soul glowing inside the trunk of the Trenynn as she settled in for a winter's nap.

I'd wake her soul again in the spring, now that I knew the tune. I looked down at the Elder flute, my fingers fluttering over the holes. Knowing clicked into place.

"Pox, plague, and blight be!" Bill lept to the side and down to a roll, coming up to stab at the tabby in the face. "A geas on thee," he spat.

The tabby in question had landed with an unusually loud thud — smoke streaming now from his nostrils as hackles rose. Elliot swatted the swiping needles of the Bloodybell to the side with one clawed paw. The sound he made deep in his chest after was more tiger-roar than hissing tom, and I began to suspect Elliot had been pulling one over on the lot of us.

"Yes, I do think," I shot back at his felt remark — an arrogant approximation of a *Ya think?* mixed with a *Well duh?* Where did he get the sass? Oh right, cat — or something like. "And he's a…" I started to say *friend*, but I wasn't sure about that. "Well, he's okay," I finished.

"A fine ally," St Germain supplied, close behind, "at the very least."

"One seeking shelter from the darkness blight we find ourselves surrounded in." The murder-hobo's bony teeth grinned menacingly as he spread hands in truce.

I looked outside for the first time since the tunnel. Desolate fog was all I could see. It blanketed everything — muting the world that still passed by, ignorant of the unknown shapes swirling in the amorphous grey. My head hurt as I tried to discern the phantasmal depths of the coincident abyss.

A bright spot against the gloom appeared — lifting the pervasive dread nagging at the back of my soul. Hearing at last the most charming little garbage disposal noises I feared forevermore absent, relief flooded me.

"Tony!" I gleed and ran for my furry little long-boi, falling to my knees as he leapt for my arms. "Thank the gods you're safe." I clutched him tightly, nearly throttling him as he ground out a protest. "Okay, okay," I relented, feeling his reciprocated relief.

"Touching," the Bloodybell drolled from the door. "I'll not note the flagrant differences in our respective welcomes," he said, smoothing an eyebrow that had apparently been singed. "Instead, I shall simply rejoice at your survival."

"How kind," I shot up an eyebrow. Had the murder-hobo hit his head in the crash?

"No kindness to it," his tone flat and simple. "Were you unalive, I'd miss my chance at the charlatan's heart." He really needed a new menacing gesture to punctuate his threats. The claw flexing was getting old.

Though as he did, I noticed one less pointed than the others. His left horn, as well, looked cracked and splintered and no small measure of crooked. The Bloodybell had not come away from the tunnel unscathed.

Neither had Tony.

"Oh, poor baby," I cooed, stroking his admittedly dingy white fur. "You chipped your beak? How awful," I said, examining him by the floating lantern's light — suddenly flaring blue as a second hurked fireball flew too close to my face, immolating a lurching bit of coalescing fog.

"Care to continue this heartwarming reunion inside?" Marty asked from the doorway. He'd picked Elliot up and was presently sweeping the cat across the fog like a loaded weapon. "Getting a bit contentious out here."

"If you safety your cat," I laughed, "sure." Elliot bristled a bit.

"He's not a cat," Marty smiled, turning to let us in — eyes scanning the fog for further incursion.

"No shit," I laughed, scratching the apparently not-a-cat behind his ears as Tony and I came inside.

Later on, I texted Felix the polymorph cat meme — captioning it simply *Elliot?*

We all have our secrets.

"Contain him! Lay his way," a timekeeper agitated.

"He wrongly thinks he controls his vantage," another calmed.

"Primed now for the side-track," the third assured.

"Yes," the last smiled, "time to derail."

Crackling wings carried me past the train bound for the mountain tunnel. Belching smoke mixed in with the wind and rain stung my eyes — my goggles doing jack and squat to help. Lenny liked the rain — called it down wherever he went. Gave him a bad rap is being gloomy.

"Oh come on," I drifted, pulling off my shades to slip on my glasses to see through the sudden downpour — a cumbersome maneuver as I drove slick roads. I still hadn't figured out how to fix my eyes in the twist, just the looks. Fine adjustments were more difficult — if I'd needed glasses with the face I wore, I was stuck with them.

Rain pelted the T-bird's windshield all of a minute before it slacked into sunshine again — right as I got my eyes swapped.

"Seriously?" Thunder laughed in my brain. "Asshole," I cursed my car as we raced along the tracks.

"Closer," I called to the Thunderbird giving me a ride. "I need to make a withdrawal." Lenny's top speed was much faster than a speeding locomotive and had superior handling.

I'd gotten word a gold shipment from a new claim deep in the La Plata Mountains was being hauled to Denver — one that struck me as suspicious in an area thought tapped out after the rush at the turn of the century. Great cover for an alchemist laundering a new batch, and I wanted a taste.

"This is a one-time thing," Lenny grumbled like distant thunder. He'd been entirely indignant at the idea of giving anyone a ride, but it was the only way to get the gold sneaky-like.

"Wanna bet?" I grinned like a madman.

Spoiler: he did, and I can always win. Let's just say Lenny has a fondness for gambling, and I've got no problem with that.

Time glitched as I bumped along the turbulent...road? Goggles, glasses, goggles again as my eyes kept swapping 'tween scenes of a trundling train to be robbed and flickering neon lights doing the robbing and the smell of spent powder connecting both. It blurred...

Back in the driver's seat, we raced along, weaving along the flat desert highway as Elvis got all shook up in the T-bird's passenger seat.

Couldn't be late to Bunny's wedding.

Not when I'd finally found *him* again.

The Wedding of Bunny Rose

THE SENSATION OF A .22 shoved in your face is remarkably the same whether it's a pearl-handled Derringer or, in this case, a rifle. Unlike the Derringer, the rifle hadn't been fired.

Bunny held it on me. Yes, *that* Bunny. Well, different body, same Bunny.

She went by another name at the time, but I'll just stick to calling her Bunny for the sake of clarity — what little can be had.

I mean, all this body hopping gets pretty confusing — even for me, and I was the one doing the hopping. Long story short — people are people, no matter the skin they wear. This Bunny wore the skin of a rancher's daughter on the outskirts of a would-be ghost town.

Shiloh grew in the last great gold boom post-La Plata strike in the mountains of Colorado, where I hoped to find the cause of my pain — and retribution. I'd find neither if she blew my head off — or at least it'd be mighty delayed.

It's times like these you have to check how your luck is working.

"Now," I began my gambit, "I imagine you have a right clear idea of whose head you want to blow off, and I don't think it's mine," I smiled. I wanted to do something as audacious as slide the barrel away from my face with the back of my hand — you know, like they do in the old...well, not yet...movies — but something told me she'd just fire anyway.

"You're the one standing on my porch, looking all smug city slick, without so much as an invitation." She pressed the barrel forward — steel tickling my nose. "I told you people we ain't selling."

Ah.

"Well, ain't buying," I assured.

"Then who is you?" She squinted closer, barrel up under my nose now.

"Name's not important," I offered none, "just a traveler who's a might lost. Can you tell me what time it is?"

"Time?" She scrunched up her face and looked up at the sun to judge. Time to press it. I tried to flip the rifle from her grip while she was squinting blind — too slow.

CLICK, pause, CLICK.

I flinched. No boom.

CLICK again.

She shoved the misfired rifle even harder in my face.

"Now ya done it," she yelled, pulling the trigger again. "Dag-blasted thing," she spat, pulling it back to examine.

"I mean you no harm, honest." I tried to appear harmless. Non-threatening.

"You just tried to steal my gun 'n turn it on me!" She menaced me further with the malfunctioning weapon.

"Well," I shrugged, "I just did what any reasonable person would'a done — they had a gun pulled on 'em. Look," I did step forward this time, nudging the barrel aside. "Just looking for a preacher-man I heard tell is in these here parts." I didn't mention him being a murderer. Or a cultist. Or an asshole.

"Pastor Finley?" She took a step back, looking me up and down again — her rifle thankfully lowered. "You lookin' to get hitched?" she asked, taking in my 'city slick' as she'd put it — fit for a wedding. "Or buryin' someone?"

"Second," I said. "He's done the marrying once before," I lied, flashing my ring.

I left out the part about it being him I'd bury. She might try to shoot me again depending on her particular feelings toward the evil son of a...

Anger flashed red in my sight, outlining my Dena's beautiful face — lifeless and vacant as she sat beneath our wedding tree.

How many times had I stared at that painting — the wedding gift she'd put her heart and soul into — watching the seasons come and go. The memories of the happy years leading to our nuptials called to mind with each lovingly crafted scene.

Every damn day I'd holed up at Sassy's redneck pagoda, I stared at it. Studied it. Relished the happiness and lost myself to the pain of their absence — drinking my troubles away. Square on the wall in full view of my favorite chair I'd pulled up the mountain solely for that purpose. Torment and bliss all wound up into one.

"I'm hoping one day I'll find a fella for him to hitch me to," Bunny sighed, breaking me out. "Or him find one for me," she added. "He's good at that, you know. Matching people up. Makes sure we all got good strong men to guide us," she eyed me up again. "An sure you already know."

"Right," I didn't commit. "Hard to believe you have trouble finding a guy," I didn't quite lie. I just knew Bunny's tastes lay elsewhere and wondered if she knew that this life.

"Now mister," she riled, "don't go startin' nothing you can't — or shouldn't," she eyed my ring, "finish."

"Not startin'." Hands up, innocent face affixed. "Just observin'."

"Mhmmm," she doubted. She turned — a little provocatively — inviting me inside. "Like what you see?" Smokey eyes turning on their allure — Bunny's always Bunny.

I didn't respond as I crossed her threshold. The well-kept small house spoke volumes of her then mindset. Practical, nothing truly personal — all items of necessity left for all to see. A curious corner of a floor rug flipped up, however, revealing what looked to be a secret beneath — one to be sussed later. For now, I followed to the small table and tea.

Her flirtatious gambit failed, she asked: "So who needs layin' to rest?"

"My wife," I said, my thumb caressing our wedding band.

Eyes wide, her mouth shut. Bravado deflated, Bunny pulled whisky from the cabinet without even being asked.

They just don't get it, I swiped. *Sure it's safe — I mean, hello, dragon guarding his book-hoard?* That had been surprising even for recent values of surprise. Marty worked for Elliot overseeing the dragon-cat's cherished collection. *But you. Aren't. There.*

Safe or not, doesn't matter. The Last Chance had been *safe*, mostly. But there, too, no Felix. So we were off to the next-to-last place he'd been seen.

Through deepening dense fog swirls and layers upon layers of grey, the diminishing streetlights failed to keep at bay. Even the lantern's blue light failed further than three feet away. It hadn't been the *best* idea in the world — everyone had told me so, volumetrically — but what other choice was there?

You know it's bad when the murder-hobo is the only one on your side. But then, he's after your heart, so...did I mention that? Oops,

I might've forgotten to mention that part. Oh well, cat's out of the bag now. Lighting shit on fire and everything.

"Shouldn't we have brought the cat?" Bill snicked sparks into the night, sharpening his broken claw and searching for lurkers bumping about — checking, too, for paths to trod. I don't recall ever seeing the murder-hobo *anxious*.

"Elliot wouldn't leave his hoard." I'd tried to coax him along, but he was having none of it. Stubborn cat. At least he'd agreed to keep an eye on Tony for me — so long as he didn't eat any books.

Poor baby'd been banged up worse than he'd let on — if a snake had a limp, that's how Tony moved once the adrenaline wore off. Plus he'd scraped off a long stretch of his soft fur — the skin attached to it — in the crash, leaving a wicked scab along his back where he'd protected me.

So, I made him stay at Lenore's where it was safe.

Save it. I know. I know.

Not hypocritical — I'm a grown-ass woman, and he's a baby. I know the risks. I also know his Mama would snackle me up if something happened to him.

"Wonders upon wonders, a world full of them. Dragons disguised as cats, trees walking like people." St Germain peered through the fog a bit nervously — his swagger and cocksure can-do attitude had waned of late, pontificating aloud to allay nerves. He stuck close to me and the blue lantern light. It hadn't shifted shades once since we left Lenore's — meaning *something* was keeping pace.

"The taxonomical name may not be your own," he went on, "but you have to admit it certainly fits. Obfirmatis, obstinate, same *stubborn* root." He laughed, winking at his joke.

I sighed and rolled my eyes. *He's from a different time,* I reminded myself. He meant nothing by it. Vaguely in the distance, I saw our destination — a shadowed outline in the fog.

"But it does explain your architectural arousal," he plod on. I grit my teeth. "I must confess, I'd never heard of such until the dear boy wrote about it in..."

"Look," I turned on the blithering alchemist. "Felix made that shit up *for* the book," and I'd already given him more than a piece of my mind for it. What's published is published, but I'd be damned if I let the rumors propagate.

"Dear girl," St Germain held out a stopping hand. I cut him off at the pause.

"He lies," I knew, "says so right in the pages." I huffed and turned back to the flatiron just in time to stop face-to-face with a giant spider — probably exiled from Australia for eating pets — stretched in a web not two inches from my face.

It shrieked at me and rattled in its web.

I shrieked back, tumbling on my ass.

"What kind of hell-spider rattles like bones?" I scrabbled away as it lobbed a sack full of splashing black acid at my feet. At least, I assumed it was acid — the ground sizzled and smoked, curling into a shadowed mass — I didn't stick around to run a litmus test.

The alchemist hurried forward, vial coming to hand. He snapped the top open and sloshed the contents at the web — the distinct stench of the stuff he called naphtha curled the hairs in my nose. In return for his flamboyant gift, the shrieking spider hurled caustic darkness in his face.

Luckily in time, he flung up his arm shand turned to the side, catching the worst of it on his coat. He cringed and cried out as the corrupting darkness began burning down to his skin, ripping the contaminant cloth away.

"The flame, dear girl," he tossed me the cigarette case already in his hand. "Strike the flame!"

The smooth metal slipped in my hand — at once too solid, yet entirely irreal, threatening intangibility — as I felt for the striking rod. Too clever by far, St Germain's handicraft refused to give up its secrets.

"How?" Fingers frantically fumbling, the case finally slid apart to reveal the source of the alchemist's flame as the warped web thrummed, signaling the spider's next putrescent volley.

I rolled away, sparking purple flame to life in my hand as I came up to a crouch. The horrid creature reared, rattling again in the now dripping web, ready to strike out — shadow boiled around it as wave after wave of evil roiled in the occluded air.

Small as it was, the flame in my hand burned bright — like the case, far denser than it had any right to be. A simple flick was all it took, setting the vile corruption alight as the alchemist fire caught in the naphtha-soaked web.

"My young, my young!" the spider wailed in terrible grief, flinging a spun sack from the conflagration as it was consumed by violent flame. It screamed, oh how it screamed, until cut short by the snick and crunch of the Bloodybell's stab.

"What the hell, Bill? You were supposed to scout!" I crawled to the Count's side as he groaned, the pain of the acid burns evident, and took out my phone, trying to see how deep the noxious substance had gone.

"It passed me over," the diminutive killer scoffed, "and bothered me not. That you failed to follow suit is no fault of mine." He'd walked right under it. "But now we have trouble tenfold as thanks," he grimaced, peering into the deeper fog.

Purple blaze lit the night, racing along the strung strands — burning sight into the mists that stared back.

Glimmers and glimpses of reflected alchemist's light, blinking in the ripples of a dozen eyes or more.

Terror and thought caught in my throat as I swiped out a simple text: *Help.*

And prayed.

CLICKsnick

"What's that?" One spun.

"Who's there?" Another.

"It's nothing, just the tin snipping," the third assured.

In darkness, deep eyes watched unseen as time passed in drips and drams.

Bunny's wedding was a fancy affair for an elopement. Plush little patio with a nice vining arch — all lit with candles and stars. Bells rang in the chapel nearby on the auspices of the occasion. Empty chairs for the guests who wouldn't be attending — but they formed an aisle lined with white roses for the bride to walk down. Bunny herself wore a curvaceously cut white tux that showed off, well, everything I tried not to look at as I stood by her side at the little altar — sudden best man and all.

In contrast, her bride wore black lace and tulle — I think that's the word — and some feathers covering her bouncing chest that seemed to be held on only by glue and the grace of the gods. It poofed at the skirt quite diaphanously, giving the appearance she floated on smoke as she came down the aisle.

"Well," I grimaced inside upon closer inspection, "shit." Odd how time gives you perspective. Then, I was saying it because of how stunning the bride-to-be looked in the ethereal dress — now, I knew better and understood what happened next when then I'd been fair flummoxed.

It *was* smoke swirling at her feet. Ravens attended the illusory train flowing behind as Misha stormed toward me — Lenny'd've been proud of the thunderhead her face became, but he was idling outside for the getaway — top down, cans affixed, sign propped on the bumper. I'd barely noticed the shift at the time or that it was because of me. Clueless as *I* was, Bunny was entirely oblivious as she jumped her bride.

"Vagina huuuugggggggs!" Bunny gleed, leapt, and — in a bizarre feat of acrobatics — wrapped her legs around the statuesque lady Fair — shoving Misha's face against the tattooed butterfly and vine.

The stripper and the elf — I knew them both — and what a pair. What stars aligned for this happenstance?

Misha glrmed and mrphed — arms waving as she tried to breathe. Her ravens grocked in protest, flapping their wings as their charge shoved Bunny away.

"What's wrong Mish-Mish?" Bunny looked at her bride, holding her face tender as she stepped down from the... vagina hugs? She tried to lock eyes with her lover, but the lady Fair had only eyes for me.

"Rose, love," she began when she could breathe again — was that her name? — "what in the name of gods old and new is *he* doing here?" Her gaze never budged, even as veins bulged. I felt myself shift uncomfortably — unsure then where the animosity had come from.

"Well," Bunny Rose looked a little hurt, "Felix here's my best man. He saved me from those nasty men your daddy sent at the motel and gave me a ride," she explained, leaving out the attempted hijacking part — probably for the best. "And!" She bounced with unbridled excitement. "He found us an Elvis to get us hitched!!"

"Uh-un-huh," Elvis swaggered in, right on cue. "That's right, little lady," the King began, "you've got the genu-wine article righ-chere to sing in your wedded bliss." He flipped his lapels up, flashing a toothy smile — showering everyone with bright sparkles of light seeming to come from nowhere. No wonder he always wore sunglasses.

"*Felix?*" The bride's mouth twisted as she said my name, venom lathering her lips. "He's calling himself *Felix* now?" Elvis ignored, her eyes veritably spat at me.

"You know Mish-Mish?" Bunny, her Rose, turned the question on me.

At the time, no. And said as much.

"I can't recall having the pleasure," I didn't lie — exactly. I tried my most charming smile in hopes of disarming this ticking time bomb.

"You can't rec..." Her mouth worked furiously. White knuckles clutched at the swirling smoke, hiking her dress as she stalked forward. Misha came nose to nose with me as I froze in place.

"Hi?" I tried for polite as her eyes bore deep into mine, casting their gaze into who I was to remember.

"Don't think I don't see you in there, *Felix,*" she put extra vitriol on my name, seeing the me that watched behind my own eyes, "and don't think I don't know what you've done." She huffed. "Coward, I call you. Coward and reprobate, you vile wretch," she really let me have it. "Return what was stolen us, and mayhap you may rest, forgiven, and the tree yet will live. *May.*"

The magnetic pull of her gaze snapped near audibly as she spent no small effort of will to break contact. Riled ravens punctuated her unsteady exit — anger and sheer spite no doubt fueling her getaway.

"Mish?" A hurt and confused Bunny Rose ran after her bride, sparing a few daggers for me along the way. "Mishaaaaa!"

That final bit of the lady Fair's tirade smacked of omen and augury — both of which I was mighty tired of.

"What tree?" Past me wondered while I knew — it was a threat.

No respite. No respect. No rest.

We ran. Ran through the closing fog.

"Pox, plague, and blight be," Bill bounced about the edges stabbing, "on thine house and thee," slitting, "on yer beasts an' barns," and skewering the smaller blobs to fling into the gaping maws of the large — distracted with morsels of their own kind. "And yer bairns."

Our lives were in the sharp hands of this curse-spitting Bloodybell.

St Germain was unable to do much more than keep upright — whatever corruption the spider'd flung had begun to spread. His burns black and dying, necrotic veins spread into healthy flesh. Out of the fight, he'd transferred a few goodies of the explosive variety to me in case of emergency — in a badass bandolier, no less — but mostly I used a stick.

Which presently propped open the slavering jaws of something nasty cartoon style. Aren't I the clever one? To be fair, my stick hadn't been that short when I'd started swinging it at the coalescing fog, but break by crack by bite, the creatures shredded it to a stub.

"Thank you, kin mine," I whispered, bidding said stub farewell as it shattered into a spray of splinters — like I'd soon be. Ah well. It'd been a nice life among the breathers, short though it was.

Blue flashed before my eyes, reminding me of the skies when I first awoke. It'd been a lovely spring day when my mother had whispered the last of the secrets among my branches.

"Back in the fight, dear girl," the stricken Count of St Germain groaned as he pulled me from beneath the lifeless lump that had gnawed my friend stick — its mouth now gummed with frothing blue foam. "We've a ways to go." The alchemist wasn't out of tricks yet, it would seem.

Stamina, though...the Count held close as I rose, his strength waning — probably couldn't run for much longer.

"Bill!" Time for the Bloodybell to take a walk. "Any way to where we like?"

"Not yet," he stabbed the coalescing mist, killing the corrupt before it could even take shape. "On hearthen stone," he resumed his curse spitting, "and the stone of yer cairn!" His tone didn't give me much hope.

I hoisted St Germain higher on my shoulder, shuffling him along in the light of the blue lantern — it seemed to give him a little strength. Whatever magic he'd worked for me seemed to help him as well.

"Shouldn't, you know," I gestured vaguely to his festering burn, "your immortality kick in soon?"

He coughed in place of a laugh, though I saw it light in his eyes and turn up his cheeks.

"Not quite so immortal anymore, dear girl." His haggard smile waned, wilting a bit.

"A path to walk," Bill slipped from sight — there then suddenly, just not. "You!?" His words cut short and before I could ask who, he came tumbling back, rolling to my feet.

His bloody red cape covered his face, briefly reminiscent of our first dreadful maize meeting.

Newly soaked, red puddled where he lay unmoving — uncursing. He wasn't faking this time.

Through the rip he'd been flung back came thick, boiling black — deeper and darker than the coincident, diffuse grey that so far blocked our way.

"The clear one," the alchemist pawed at the vials in the nifty bandolier. "Throw it so the invisible alights," he made no sense. Maybe the festering had fevered? "Then, the blue before we do, too."

"What?"

"With haste," he slumped, urgent energy expended.

Great. Just great. My mind spun. My hand grabbed the vials of clear and blue. No further instruction, I just did, flinging the clear to shatter at the split in the world.

Nothing happened.

Not that I could see anyway, but I heard.

Heard the howl and rush of sudden wind as the dread black caught alight in orange flame. It writhed as it burned, collapsing to ash as more flames leapt into the air, revealing dozens and dozens of — things — I had no name for lying in wait.

"Blue," the alchemist rasped, his breath thin. My head grew light — I was finding it hard to breathe as well, my lungs feeling aflame. "Blue..."

Fumbly fingers found their way to the stoppered concoction, but only managed to dislodge the vial.

Gravity did the rest.

How kind, I thought distant as glass shattered at my feet.

Diamonds leapt and sparkled, clearing whatever the first vial had unleashed, burning the air to ash and hissing vapor. Soot rained down, showering the figure emerging from the distant rip.

Hooded and cloaked, face obscured, it strode toward us with uncanny silence. If I didn't see the shadow, I'd never know anyone was there.

"My, my," a radiant voice tsked. "What a mess," she — I felt reasonably certain, I knew the voice — sighed.

More figures coalesced from the path opening behind her. I slumped to my knees in disbelief.

Our escape — and fate — sealed.

Plain and simple. It was my fault — again — that someone I cared about had got hurt, maybe even dead by now. I'd been gone too long in this trap of a life twice lived.

I sulked at the open bar — past me was just enjoying a drink after the chaos, but I was benefiting. Strangely, I recalled feeling a sudden melancholy as I sipped my whisky, unsure why. Just a feeling. An inkling.

I guess I should pay more attention to those. Tune in to the varying mes.

Maybe all the knowledge we ever need or will know is right there in the back of our brains, tickling at our neurons — begging for us to just *listen* for once. But I was drunk and thinking drunk things.

I half expected Sassy to roll in to pick up Elvis — a drunk Felix and open bar were like mating calls to the legend. We'd already been gone longer than planned, and the big ape tended to worry. He'd already given me enough grief about borrowing Elvis to begin with — the King wasn't too keen on the idea either.

"Now just a minute, butter-britches," Elvis protested, still wearing his bathrobe. "You want me to do a what now?"

"Wedding." I pulled one of his most dazzling jumpsuits from the closet. "All the rage in Vegas."

"Now I know I owe you, champ," he uh-un-huned with a swaggering hand, "but I'm no preacher-man. No-oh."

"Well, all the ordained Elvi have been banned in sin city," I tossed him the glitz and rummaged some sunglasses, "thanks to *someone's* estate," I side-eyed the King. "And the black-market ones are all booked up."

"Uh-un-huh," he reflexively sang.

"Pretty big marker you're calling in for this Bunny-girl," Sassy sassed, leaning against the door frame — watching the commotion.

I scrubbed hands through my hair, unsure. "In over my head before I knew it," I explained. "Plus, I got the feeling," I scratched an itch that wouldn't, "that I owed her."

I did kill the preacher at her wedding — well, less of a wedding, more of a virgin sacrifice thing, but I'll get to that in a minute.

"Mhmm," Sassy pursed his lips. He wanted to say more, but refrained. He was surprisingly tight-lipped when he wasn't drinking. Reserved, even. Go figure.

"I'll have him back by sunrise," I promised. Bunny and her bride were absconding in the middle of the night on my — I forget how many days I'd been awake by that point in my misjudged life — let's say, third night in Vegas. That whole trip was disastrous.

"First the painting, then the Thunderbird, now Elvis — what else of mine do you want? Shall I disconnect and pack up the kitchen sink for you as well?" He'd flipped his Farrah hair and made with the melodrama.

"I just gave you the painting for safe-keeping while I was, er," I hedged, thinking of the proper descriptor for stalking death's door, "indisposed. And after, well, it *belonged* in a museum." Elvis and assorted accouterments acquired, I moved the conversation along out the door where the T-bird in question sat idling. "And Lenny'd needed a totem to inhabit, so that wasn't my fault." It had been a whole thing — long story — but, like I said, totally *not* my fault. The engine revved impatiently.

"This isn't Sassy's Self-Storage, you know," he huffed. Sassy-pants had more than a few of my things tucked amongst his bric-a-brac — some he wasn't even aware of.

"I know." I felt bad for taking advantage of his propensity to collect things — and people — to slip my own treasures among his. "But there's no one I'd trust more with what's important," I said in earnest, then began bundling Elvis into the T-bird's passenger seat.

"Hoa now, jelly-hips," Elvis stopped — that one didn't even make sense. "You got any sandwiches in that speed-rod?"

I froze, forgetting to pack a snack. The King's appetite was prodigious, and he was entirely food motivated. I'd never get him to the wedding without some caloric enticement.

Sassy-pants saved the day yet again, holding out a brown-bagged lunch for the King to munch. "Be careful," Sassy fretted. "You know your luck with weddings."

"This won't be like last time," I'd assured him from across the T-bird, long before I knew who Bunny was set to marry.

Seeing Misha in the dress — stalking down the aisle, ready to punch my face in — had been a total surprise. Even more surprising was what she said as she sat next to me at the open bar.

"Last time I saw you," she began, "was at death's door." The ferocity of her stare made me itch. Gone was her gown of wedding black and the ravens. In their place were comfy sweats and yoga pants stained with some sort of dip.

"Well, I guess I got better," I'd laughed, not knowing how true it was — just trying to lighten the mood.

"You really don't remember." It wasn't a question so much as an admission — mostly to herself.

"Hasn't bubbled up yet," I'd shrugged, answering anyway. There'd seemed to be no point in making shit up — and I was already drunk — so why not see where this led. "Can you stop staring at me so hard? Please?" It'd become more than uncomfortable.

This bought me some riotous, bitterly tinged laughter from the lady Fair. Tears, too, as she turned her head away, cracking her neck frozen stiff and looking toward the vacant heavens. She shivered and shuddered, pleasure seeming to ripple through her.

"There," she sighed, warmth now in her eyes, "was that so hard?"

There it was again, that feeling I'd done something unwittingly clever — bleeding through from past me to present. If I had half a notion what I was really doing...

"Am I late?" A bouquet of flowers filled the doorway — ostentatious wasn't enough of a word to describe it. If lavish, copious, and luxurious chipped in, they might live up to the floral swank. "Fashionably so, I hope," said the bouquet with a voice I now well recalled.

"Perfectly on time," Misha sparkled, her diaphanous gown twisting once more into place from the ether as she passed the bloom-laden Count of St Germain. "Over there, if you please," the lady Fair addressed the flowers.

Vines trailing down from the overgrown nosegay sprang to life, startling the Count into losing his grip on the greenery as it traipsed where directed upon new-grown legs.

"Oh! M'lady," St Germain swept a courtly bow, presenting the bride with a gold-wrapped box retrieved from somewhere or other — about his person, within the twist, from some contrived dimension of pockets — I wasn't sure exactly what tricks the alchemist knew. We all have our mysteries.

"A most gracious gift," Misha nodded approvingly — seeming to know what the box contained without even opening it. "My thanks," she said, plucking a black feather from her dress, presenting it to the immortal in trade for the gilt box.

St Germain playfully twisted the feather twixt his fingers, smiling as the black shimmered. "You didn't tell me this was a Fair Folk affair!" He leaned against the bar in the spot Misha had vacated. I was still on my third whisky, soon to be fourth.

"I didn't tell you it was any sort of affair. What are you doing here?" He'd seen the note Bunny'd slipped me, but I hadn't shared the details — hell, I didn't *know* any *to* share. I'd just met him a few hours before, and though he remembered me, I had fuck-all clue about who he was or if he was what he claimed. No, I wasn't going to invite him to a wedding I'd been conscripted as best man for — as such, it *was* purportedly my job to keep out the riff-raff.

"The young lady invited me," he smiled, running the feather under his nose like a fine cigar, closing his eyes as he inhaled the scent.

"Kind of her," *undermining my job like that,* I grimaced, words unspoken. A thought struck. "She gave me your note, though."

"Ah! Wonderful," the Count smiled. "Should help keep your pockets lined without all the fuss of unnecessary gambling," he waved, dismissive of my skill. "Why I remember when you used to get run out of taverns every night," he laughed, "and TWICE on Sundays!" The Count continued his examination of the feather, waxing reminiscent — balancing it on the tip of his finger. "You'd pull some stunt or other," he shifted his eyes to me, "*cheating* as you so love to say," his lips curled to smile. "Last I checked, dear boy, your faces are *still* prominent in the banned books at Royal Ascot. A few others as well," his eyebrows waggled in delight. "All these years upon years later."

"I just have a knack for it," I'd played along, no clue what he was on about. I felt the years he spoke of now, etching again in memory. Highlights, at least.

"For trouble, certainly." He tippled a flask procured from where I wasn't looking.

"Can you teach me that?" I'd felt it was something I should know how to do.

St Germain laughed. Spit-take levels of laughter. "Dear boy," he relented when he saw I was asking in earnest. "That's one of the tricks *you* taught *me*."

Oh. I forget what I forgot sometimes.

"But certainly, dear boy," the alchemist said, meeting my gaze — the me inside, second in as many to do so. "I've much to show you."

And did.

"*Time unwinds round again,*" *a timekeeper full of fret frayed.*

"*Unstuck,*" *another.*

"*Unfair!*"

"*Cheater,*" *the last laughed.*

I always cheat.

Cards. Dice. All the games you can name.

Taxes and Death, as well, the two less certain about me.

Until I lose, I can always win.

There was one time, though, I lost, and lost dearly. I didn't much like that.

But the fool's key away in my hand, safe under a worrying eye, gave me the chance to fix it — gave me time to get it right.

Turn the key. Rewind the scene, riotous in reverse.

Dust sucked into the tires as Lenny unpeeled out, rattling cans leading the way back — bounding and hopping, drawing the Thunderbird along like tiny silver sled dogs. Misha's green scarf stabbed the air violently as the newlyweds returned — lashing about in wild fury.

Their lips unlocked as the brides turned to face back to us, away from the sinking dawn.

"Denrae nib-sah, diap-ecyrp. Denruter won, nevig't fig-a." The new Mrs. Bunny Rose jerked her hand back and forth, adieu unbid. Her arm and elbow awkward, strangely bent. She reached for the glovebox, replacing the fine leather gloves that matched her scarf upon her hands, lowering her shades with relaxed fingers tipped in speckled pink.

"Nawrou folla, shrutnevdawn-oot," bright hiccups of laughter swallowed down, smiles chewing the ebullient cheer.

Out of the car they leapt. With a shift and a twist, Misha wore again her smoky black gown, her getaway greens slipping away. Magically to hand, her bouquet was recalled from the Count of St Germain.

The door burst shut as we made our way back through grains of unthrown rice — the spectators the chapel had paid sucked in their ebullient cheer, repossessed for another day.

Suory nub srssim dn srssim tneserp on-i," the King declaimed, his hand descended. "Edirb eh zik yamu," his lip uncurled.

Rings slipped from fingers, at the little white altar we stood, the spot my mind began to fray.

"Ood eya," my tears unshed.

Mercurial Edge

LIFETIME AFTER LIFETIME, SPLICED into one before my eyes as Elvis read the vows…I drifted from Bunny's wedding to my own.

My wedding, step once to the left and I found myself in Bunny's place. St Germain in mine.

He'd been my best man then and three more. Charged with keeping us safe. Having my back, not stabbing it.

I stared down at the man who betrayed me, let them steal the one I loved so dear, my Dena. Ripped her soul away to keep, unprayed. So tempted the chicken had been when he saw her, I should have known.

We all should have. Hank had warned us. Said he was *off*. Rotten where we could not see. But we are all given our mistakes to make. Our consequences to take.

It's so clear now from that place between dreaming and wake, cut loose from the bonds of reality, where time matters not — gelatinous as it truly is. The true stuff of dreams manifest.

I blamed him for a long time — my best friend, best man — the immortal alchemist should have chosen his would-be acolytes better. Even if the chicken'd never been initiated to the Mysteries, he knew of their existence, knew of their power. Should have trusted Hank, devil's details.

Easy to say now, but then I was a terror in my grief. My heart grew dark inside my chest, living the moment over and over again — vacant eyes flashing before mine whenever their heavy lids shut.

"How *could* you!" I slugged, sending the Count of St Germain sprawling across the island sands. My rage pent for years, finally leeching loose. "You *hid* that..." I seethed.

Gone, the one who tempered it. Ripped away from me by cruelty and ignorance — the latter mine. It was my fault.

Hank was right.

"Dear boy," he began, his lip starting to swell. "It is my most grievous sin and one I am desperate to correct." Being immortal did not inure him to pain. "But more, I try to prevent more grievous harm that cannot be undone."

"I don't care your intent," I railed, "only the deeds done!"

My mind reeled. His had not been the hand that had done the deed, but he'd hid that hand after the fact — sworn that he, too, had been betrayed by the Black Pullet. Yet he concealed the culprit and misled my search.

I'd come close in West London, dueling the renewed Pullet on the steps of the Dawn's Blythe Road headquarters. The coward ran, giving me the slip. Across the continent, I searched, the new world, too, and nothing.

Until I tasted the gold.

In truth, I'd been looking for the Pullet's among the bootleggers and suspicious mother-loads — and found it. But there was a subtle flavor shift amongst the coins.

The aurum produced by each practitioner was similar — the basic recipe is the same handed down since the times of the Thrice Great — but each subtly different. St Germain added a splash of panache — in everything he did, really — while the Black Pullet tainted everything he touched, imparting an acrid tang with hands stained by so much blood.

St Germain's unique recipe shone through — the subtle bitterness of the bay leaves betraying his mixed in with the chicken shit.

I'm getting off track again — it's been harder for me to focus of late. There's been static in my thoughts. Anyway, let's go back to the caves.

Bunny's wedding wasn't a fancy affair that first time. Rather modest and humble — or it would have been. You see, it was to be a mass wedding put on by the preacher-man named Finley, so he lied, to bring happiness and joy through the sanctity of marriage, he defiled.

Yeah, I'd stuck around the town longer than planned. Made up some bullhockey to feed Bunny and the rest while I sussed some truth out. Even burned some old bones I'd found to fill an urn — I'd said I was there to bury my wife and all. Needed a body to keep up appearances.

Or something like that.

I don't really remember all the lies I've told. Writing them down helps, but when you've told so many, they're bound to come unraveled with time. Crisscrossed in the stitch, one grafted to another. But some moments are clear as crystal, permanently etched in my psyche.

The Black Pullet was not what I expected in the slightest. Bent and stooped, white hair straggly and falling out. He looked a corpse himself in his funeral blacks. Time had by no means passed him by as it had the man standing to his side as he'd stood at mine.

My once friend, the traitorous Count of St Germain.

I punched him again for good measure, coming back to the island. Some things I still can't bear to watch — my mind simply slips from them. Coward.

Blood covered my hands.

What had I done?

"The cards said you'd find him," Deirdre sighed. "Lead me straight to him!"

I couldn't believe it. There she stood in the midst of the enemy corrupt — a small army of them — calm and collected as if she were having tea.

"I saw it, though, and so it shall come to pass." Her radiant positivity surfacing once more. "Even if I have to help it a little," she winked and waved the horde forward toward us.

St Germain groaned, in slightly better shape than the murder-hobo. Bill didn't stir.

The horde rolled through the grey like black fire toward our merry little band of the doomed and then burst.

They, too, caught alight — putrescence burning to crumbling cinders. In the midst of the fog, I caught faint shimmers like heat waves rippling off summer asphalt. The pavement itself became somehow wetter, with puddles forming beneath the hissing flames.

The alchemist grinned as the fortune teller scowled. "Protium phlogiston," he husked. "Added a smidgen of lithos to Cav's recipe for spice." He tried to laugh, but wheezed more.

I wasn't sure what the hell he was on about, but his flaming air had made a barrier around us the blackness couldn't cross. Whatever science-magic he'd worked, I wasn't questioning.

"Delaying the inevitable," Deirdre sighed. "You can't fight fate." She pulled the Death card from her deck. "See?" Theatric bitch.

"Shove it," I shouted. Tarot Death simply meant change. All things change. The reader was putting on yet another show — one for intimidation. She'd conned us good, it would seem. I felt so stupid, but it clicked.

Deirdre betrayed us, I texted Felix, leaving out the complexities of the cat-and-mouse con she'd run. He ought to at least know she was a baddie if he ever came back. Looked like I wouldn't be around to warn him, but these handy little boxes the breathers invented were super helpful for that. The connections they made lessened the pang of regret I felt leaving the forest's whole. Addictive, actually.

Outside the barrier of flames, I thought I heard her monologuing, but it was hard to sort out from the whoosh and hiss of the burning chattel she flung to our invisible inferno. I really didn't care to listen anyway.

Instead, I turned inward. Gathering my thoughts. I looked to the barely breathing alchemist — eyes scrunched in pain — and the unconscious Bloodybell and began to set my feelings to words.

Hey Felix, it's been a good run, but I think it's over. They *caught up to me,* I swiped and sent.

You're something else. You know that? Special. To me, I started. *To lots of people,* I added, thinking of the others — everyone who'd shown up looking for him. Except Deirdre, the traitor. She could rot. *I know you're off trying to find a fix for me or some such nonsense, but it's okay. I just wish you were here with us. There's so much I want to tell you — stuff I wish I could say in person — but I suppose a text'll have to do. I...*

Read 4:02am the ripple ran up the thread as all the messages checked.

Thought-train derailed, tears came to my eyes as the dots I'd so longed for appeared.

Thunderbolts and lightning.

The wind whipped as the sky broke, crashing down on us in a sudden burst that stung my eyes shut. I flattened myself over the wounded and felt my white hair frizz and stand on end. Ozone filled my nose.

Many storms I'd weathered in the forest, but they always put me on edge. One unlucky strike and it could all end in ash. One errant gust and boughs could break, or I'd simply topple if I were truly misfortunate. I knew the signs well.

The lightning came, but not for me — blinding the sky.

Instead, jagged bolts of gold ripped through the horde, drawing ever closer as their brethren burned — depleting the phlogiston in their attempted attrition. The world went silent as the thunder's roar noped my hearing.

My hand buzzed.

Get in!

Rage throbbed inside my head, clouding all thought.

I'd seen her, I think now but didn't know, seen her soul clear as bright day held captive in a gemstone. My Dena. I could see her essence being sucked away, one day at a time — fed into the horrid creature who wore it.

I saw it held in my mind's eye as I woke bleary, key winding again as needling light pricked my eyes. I shoved it away — slipping back under the currents.

Currents? How had that gone?

Oh yes, a river had run through the cave, strangely enough. Cavern really, cut into the cliff-side by the trickling water of millennia escaping the ground. The good people of Shiloh had gathered for the Grand Blessing ceremony — uniting the unwed of the community.

Bonfires lit the cavern at five points, bathing the stone in a red glow. Five couples to be wed stood at each while the townsfolk gathered in a circle around them.

All wore white. All were blind fools, deceived by the Pullet. In their midst, the foul thing calling himself Finley walked, hunched but voice strong. Calling out ritual blessings — speaking words in a tongue long dead — he offered a toast to seal the vows.

Poor Bunny, it was too late for her this life cut short. I slumped as they fell, celebratory wine poisoned, spilling over the cave floor. She deserved better.

The summoning ritual began and the Black Pullet would use their fresh souls for bait.

Offered to what? I wasn't sure, but it was a nasty business.

One I interrupted.

Wait... how'd it go again?

Oh yeah, I fucked up.

"She's gone!" Hank spat at me. "For good this time," he fumed, righteous in his anger.

"What are you yelling at me for?" I didn't know. "I got the gods-damned asshole who killed her!" I didn't know. "*He's* the one who hid the bastard for so damn long!" I didn't know.

"Because I *told* him to!" Hank railed. "I knew you'd screw it up, ya hot-headed fool!" Hank's eyes glowed red as he shouted, voice deepening. "You doomed her." Tears steamed from the corners of his eyes with a hellacious hiss.

"Dear boy," St Germain rose. "Matters are more complex than even you know," he tried to explain as Hank continued to seethe. "You could never find her because she never died."

"But," I deflated, "I saw her."

"Her shell only," the alchemist said gently. "Emptied."

Things began falling into place.

I'd fucked it all up.

"He remembers, but refuses," one timekeeper said.

"Broken," said another.

"Aren't we all," the third.

"He must confront," said the last.

Get. In. The message echoed, urgent in my head as I read.

"In what?" I saw nothing *to* get in.

Tires screeched faintly in my noped-out ears. Sparks and crackles flew as salvation tore through the corruption — striking it down with unerring bolts wherever it passed.

The Thunderbird skidded to a halt between us and the horde, its door flinging open.

"Thank the gods, Felix." I went to the door. "Help me with..."

The driver's seat was empty.

Get in! it repeated. Annoyed?

The voice — which I belatedly realized was in my head — did not belong to Felix.

"Not without them!" My finger shot at my prone friends. I could see the massing gloom through the window opposite — recovering from the striking lightning. Regathering.

When I turned back, St Germain was stumbling to his feet, slamming a glass vial to the ground, and lurching toward the waiting car. I grabbed Bill by the hoofed foot, dragging him none-too-gently over the road.

Wind roared around me as a gale buffeted the three of us roughly toward the T-bird. Lightning ripped at the ground around us as we piled in, sending chunks up into the monstrous faces come too close.

"Pox," Bill whispered faintly as I yanked him onto the floorboard, "plague, and blight…" He moaned, curling in on himself. I scrambled over to the driver's side to let the alchemist slump in. *Things*, nasty and sharp lunged.

I threw the car in gear and stomped the gas, gripping the wheel tight.

Easy leadfoot, the annoyed voice said. *I got it from here.*

We peeled out, doing a donut to bump a few bumpers, and took off — speed slamming the door shut along the way.

"Hey, watch it!" I yelped, bouncing and jumping in my seat as we ran over another. "You sure you know how to drive?" Ridiculous question to ask a car. I tried gripping the wheel to straighten us out, but it was apparently just for show. In the seat or not, I wasn't the one driving.

Sure do, kid, said the voice in my head, *better than you.* The nerve of this car!

"I drive just fine, thank you," I huffed, feeling argumentative for some strange reason. "Driven you all over when Felix was trashed."

Ha! The engine coughed and sputtered. Laughing? *If you did, I wouldn't. You'd'a ground my gears to shrapnel if I drove the way you try.*

A bumper shot in front of the Thunderbird, square in the high beams and growing larger. Not because we sped toward it, but *actually* grew.

Hang on, kid, the Thunderbird roared, picking up speed as the creature loomed higher, dripping foulness. I sprawled across the alchemist in the seat next to me, grabbing his belt and strapping it across, hooking an arm through my own. Bill would just have to make do down on the floor.

The true storm broke loose, wind howling as a funnel descended. Lightning shot from the front of the T-bird, crackling and shrieking as it stabbed out into the icky black. I felt the car lift off the ground and into the air as we rode into the storm.

"Madness," a timekeeper marveled.

CLICK

"Did you hear that?" the second, distracted.

rattle

"Chaos," the third, disquieted, watching the audacious scene. "Chaos incarnate."

CLICKcreak

"Seriously, what..." the second, silenced.

The fool key turned in my hand a final time. The lock come undone.

My breath stopped as a fearful hand clutched.

"You better not be…" faded away as time stretched. My eyes lingered on the painted scene, so happy before me. The tree had blossomed so bright.

I chose to be happy for a while longer.

We landed with a thump, springs groaning in protest as I'm sure we scraped bottom. But! We were in one piece — at least we were in the same number of pieces we started with, I think. The T-bird might have lost a tailpipe.

Bright side, we made it through a tornado. Somehow.

Slowly, I got out of the car — checking briefly to see if we'd landed on anything or any*one*. No curling feet, we were good — and took a look around.

Lush valley, check. High mountains on all sides. Treacherous switchback climbing to their top — half crumbled into a rock slide. Fun. Ramshackle house beside a small pond. Naturally.

The word hardly described the multilevel confabulation of wood and tin and precariously balanced bricks. I think I even spotted some structural rust in key spots as well, but it could have been stylistic distress as opposed to actual. More than anything, the structure consisted of porches of varying heights and chairs to rock in upon them.

There were even pitchers of sun tea set on some of the rails to brew — their bags swirling with lemon slices as the brilliant rays struck. Homey.

Also odd, considering we'd just been dropped in via twister from a completely cloudless sky.

"On the seed of your lands," the Bloodybell resumed his cursing, "an' labor of your hands," he bumbled and thumped, struggling to free himself from the floorboard. "Confound it!"

"Hang on, hang on!" I ran to the passenger door as it swung wide, St Germain limp inside. "Easy now, let me help." I dashed in as the Count was about to fall out, held in only by the strapped seat belt. He groaned, fumbling for the latch, trying to open his eyes.

Horror met mine as he did — the whites were completely black, pools of the spreading corruption staring at me.

"Dear girl," he tried to say, barely above a whisper. Empty pools staring distant.

"I got you." I gently cradled the not-so-immortal, clicking loose the belt. I held back sudden tears as he slid out clumsily to the ground. Frail was not a word I'd associated with the alchemist before that moment, yet now. St Germain's legs flopped to the ground as the Bloodybell ungently shoved, tumbling himself free to the grass.

"Starless night, Bill, be..." I started to chide. Cut short by a scream.

More a keening wail that ripped through the valley, freezing us all stone still. The curdling sound echoed off the mountains, shaking them to their very foundations.

"What was that?" I'd been through a dismal grey Hell the last day and a half, never once batting an eye, but at that primal cry, my knees began to quiver.

"Nothing good." The murder-hobo rose from his sprawl, scanning for enemies.

None appeared, save a figure from the house, oddly small in the doorframe. He walked with a swagger toward us as the tremors subsided, smoothing back his slick, black hair.

"Hwoah there, little lady," Elvis — was that Elvis? — un-uh-huhed, gold pinky ring flashing as he motioned me to stop. No other glitz, just the ring — pretty casual in a non-sparkly jumpsuit, but he did wear shades. "Let me give you a hand." The King came to my side, taking up the Count of St Germain as if he weighed nothing. "Haven't seen you since Vegas, sport," he addressed the alchemist. "You're looking swell," he lied a comforting lie.

Load lightened, I ran back to the Thunderbird to fetch the lantern; somehow, it got stuck in the rear window. "Where are we?"

"The Sanctuary," the King said as if I knew what that meant. I leaned into the seat to grab the floating flame, now a happy orange. I guess this place must be okay.

Ow! I barked my hip on something sharp — the glovebox door. In all the ruckus, Bill must've kicked it open. A pair of green leather gloves slipped out. Curiously, their fingers were tipped with pink. I pulled them out to look, their soft leather cool against my skin. A note fell from where it'd been tucked in between.

"C'mon, big fella's waiting for you," he said gently. "You too, little lady," he called back to me. I turned, tucking the gloves and note in my pocket — the scripted hand familiar, but I'd have to read it later.

Elvis stopped Bill short as he made to follow. "Not you." Ice laced his words to the Bloodybell, punctuated by an even colder stare over his shades.

"I go where they go, lest the given word break," the murder-hobo snapped, stabbing toward the King with pointed fingers. "I was promised that charlatan *Felix's* still-beating heart..."

"A *chance* at it," I corrected before he got any ideas.

"Well, snicker-snack, you missed your chance," he sneered, "by about two minutes, give or take."

The wailing cry.

My feet froze, heart lurching in my chest. "What?" All life drained away. It couldn't…I couldn't…

"Best let Sassafras explain," Elvis said, tender. "C'mon," he repeated.

My body followed though my world stood still.

I lazed, relaxing into her as we lay beneath our tree atop the stone statue head.

My personal heaven, respite from the world so taxing. The place we were alone and whole.

"You're needed, my love," she stroked. Always the strong one. The wise one.

"Yes," I said. "I'm needed right here." I ignored everything outside our little world.

"Of course, my love," she smiled at me. "I always need you, but I'm not alone in that."

Something was different.

I sat up straight, looking back at my Dena. She smiled her beautiful smile, and I knew I'd have to leave her again.

"I don't want to," I sulked.

"I'll be here," she said, holding my hand. Always the strong one.

I lingered in her glistening eyes.

"Oh honey," I distantly heard Sassy-pants say, enveloping me in a hug. This was his place, huh?

"No wonder we couldn't find him." I weakly laughed, too empty to ebulle. My eyes met his as I pulled back. He smirked through tears, joke dawning.

"Not the world hide-and-seek champ for nothing, sweet cheeks!" He squeezed tighter. "Come on, I'll take you to Felix."

"I thought he was..." Confused.

"You'll see," he said, leading on. Elvis came close behind, carrying the Count. "It's been getting worse and worse," Sassy explained poorly as we climbed step after step. The house was as ramshackle on the inside as it was the out — a labyrinth of add-ons and redos and cut-throughs. "He's been in and out for a while, but lately, he's just been out. And now, nothing."

Our path meandered through what was apparently the second-floor kitchen — all done in cedar shake with an open window to an inner porch. Calling it a kitchen was slightly misleading — this one had a dedicated bar with a half-dozen taps and a wall of scotch, while the actual cookery part was relegated to a corner with a toaster, electric kettle, and microwave. All you need, really.

"I'm glad you got the text," Sassy said. "Felix tried — I think — but...I had to help." I kept quiet, mind reeling — the worst possible thoughts.

Sassy grabbed a tea set ready on a tray with one hand, adding a bottle with the other. "For later." I followed, the lantern taking on a rosy glow as we walked through the darker halls.

The entire time, St Germain grew more and more restless. "The boy," he kept repeating. "Must see," he sought with near-blind eyes that kept fixing on the floating light beside me. "Must tell."

"Sure will. First in line, sport," Elvis assured. I wondered. The alchemist looked worse by the second, the corruption eating away at him, shriveling him.

"In here." Sassy stopped by the door.

I couldn't. I'd come so far, through so much, to find him. And now, he was just on the other side. But, according to Sassy, not.

Are you there? I swiped a quick text, confusing the shit out of the Bigfoot.

DING

I teared up. He never kept his phone on silent.

Smiley face.

DING

Praise hands.

DING

I couldn't help it. I laughed.

I'm coming.

DING. I creaked open the door.

On the wall, I saw the painting we'd liberated from the Doyle — what seemed like so long ago. *Spring's First Blush* lived up to the title now — tree in full pink bloom. Beneath it, I could see not a guy fishing, but a couple... well. *I* blushed, for sure, and looked away.

Down to the chair sat before the painting in full view. One of those high-backed leather ones great for sinking into, lounging. Strangely, the back was bare, showing the tufted button strings and supportive springs conforming to the shape of the occupant through the frame.

"Felix?" My heart beat faster. No shuffle, no response. "You've got a lot of people worrying, you know. Taking off like that," I filled the unbearable silence as I came 'round. "At least read your texts."

The unread phone perched on the overstuffed chair arm, threatening to fall — one buzz from a drop — and in the chair, Felix. Unmoving.

He didn't blink. He didn't breathe. I didn't think his heart even beat.

I sank to my knees in front of the chair as he stared emptily at the wall. "Oh, Felix." The lantern hovering behind me cast its warm glow on his inanimate body where it sat.

"Let me see the boy," St Germain struggled, vigor renewed. He stumbled and fell, crawling to my side. I helped raise him up to see what he could through nearly blind eyes — black veins spiderwebbing his entire face now. "Oh, dear boy," he wept, hand reaching for Felix's.

"Is there something we can do? Some elixir you can give him?" My eyes searched the alchemist for some mystical answer. Surely there had to be something. How else had the man staved off death so long?

He bowed his head and cursed. "Gone. I drank the last," he deflated. "Had I not been hit," he bit harshly. "Had I known..."

The vial he smashed. One last effort to get to the Thunderbird.

"Tell me," he straightened. Self-loathing could wait. "Describe what you see for a blind fool."

"There's not much here," I started. "The chair has no backing. His phone is on the armrest. He's really, really thin," I worried. "Almost skeletal. He's got an old clock in his lap, I think. It's hard to tell. His hands are covering it."

The alchemist's brow furrowed. "What else?"

I looked around, finding not much else. "That painting is on the wall," I said. "He's staring at it."

"Of course," St Germain smiled. "Dena's wedding present."

I never knew her name. Just that it was from his forgotten wife. Had Felix remembered?

"What day is it?"

"Monday, I think..."

"No, no," he interrupted. "In the painting, what day is showing?"

"Umm," I hedged, not sure how to describe it. "The tree is blooming, and there's two people getting it on underneath."

"Ahem," he coughed. "Well, the dear boy won't like it, but..." He laid his hand on Felix's, over the concealed clock.

"...I'm afraid I'll have to interrupt," a voice startled my inner peace.

"Damnit, Rakozy," I bolted straight up. "Don't you know how to knock?" I threw the picnic blanket over my wife.

"On what door, dear boy?" The Count laughed and made a show of searching the open outdoors. "Dena, dear," he tipped a hat he didn't wear.

"Your Highness," she smiled as if he'd just popped by for tea. "Or are you going under more common pretense now?" She quirked an eyebrow at the alchemist.

"How about simply friend?" He smiled.

"HA!" Peace spoiled, the memories of betrayal slithered in. "I call you friend no more," I glared. "Not after what you did." I placed myself more firmly between the Count and my wife.

"Dear boy," he sighed, "your memory is confabulated." Blackness filled his eyes.

"He's right, my love," my heart sighed as well. "You've come to fetch him then?" This to my betrayer.

"Fetch me?" What was happening? "No, I'll not leave you. Not again!"

"It's okay, my love," Dena. "We'll be together again."

"But I need you," I clutched her tight, my heart ripping asunder again at the thought of being without her.

"And I, you," she kissed me. "But I'm tired and in need of rest."

"I just found you again," I whined. "Why must I leave?" It hurt too much.

Dena laughed, that beautiful tittering tinkle I loved so dear. "You never lost me, silly," she sweetened. "You only lost sight of it."

"Time to be off, dear boy," St Germain laid a hand on my shoulder. "You need to set things a'right now." Corruption spread through his face, cracking and ashing his skin. "And she needs her rest," he said as she faded, tears sparkling in her smiling eyes as they, too, filled with inky black, consuming the world.

"I'll come for you," I shouted to the void between stars. "I promise! No matter how long."

Small. Distant. I heard her whisper. "I am ever patient."

Nothing.

We floated in absent abyss.

"Why?" I turned on my former friend. "I was happy!" I cried, tears shed like diamonds floating in lightless glimmer.

"You deceive yourself still, dear boy." St Germain sadly shook his head. "Stuck in a trap of your own making, but my design." Distantly, his eyes appraised. "I never imagined you'd use it so."

He clutched his chest as reality throbbed. "Quickly, I have little time."

"Funny thing for an immortal to say," I sneered, still not trusting his words.

"Not so immortal anymore, dear boy." His laugh was rueful and true, at least. "Long story short," he began. He never cut anything short. "In your hotheaded rage, you killed the Pullet..."

"And you hid him from me, you..." I took a swing.

"Stop it!" The Count dodged to the side, tripping me as I passed. "Listen. He killed your wife, you were right to be angry, but he'd tied her soul to his through the black arts."

"He what?"

"Insurance," St Germain explained. "Don't you think *Hank* wanted to rip him limb from limb more so than even you? Boil his atoms in eternal perdition? You're strong, dear boy, but Hank is far greater than you...if he'd not fallen..." He started to side-track. Fallen? "Point being he couldn't. Not without hurting Dena — which he'd never allow, so he bided."

"Why didn't you tell me?"

"You wouldn't listen, you thrice-damned fool!" The alchemist gathered his composure once more. "There was no stopping you, not then and there, not with your tricks in force. Whatever we'd have done would've turned back on our own hand. So we deceived, the devil and I."

I couldn't believe my ears. My two greatest friends, allies, conspired against me, but it rang true. Hank had punched me; I'd seen it. It hadn't gone well for him.

"And then what?" I wasn't prepared to believe, but I could listen.

"I pulled him as far from you as I could. Helped the asshole set up a *new* ritual — as much as it damned my soul."

"Why..." I started to interrupt, but he held up a hand.

"Only when he tried to reach across the abyss, tried to descend a god, only then would he make his offering, severing the soul he kept prisoner, leeched to extend his life. So we waited, Hank and I, for that one infinitesimal moment."

"And your luck ran out," I finished. Luck was always with me.

"Straight to you," he nodded. "You found him right at his weakest but struck too soon. Damn cheater."

I wanted him dead *before* he could gain power greater than mine, so I shifted things that way. Shit. "Then what?"

"I'm honestly not sure. Hank would know more than I," he admitted. "But when the Pullet died and the gem shattered, I think their souls — or that of whatever such are made — twined and twisted to something..." He pointed to the vile corruption spreading across his face.

"No wonder Hank was pissed." I sighed, heart sinking. I'd royally fucked it up.

"Indeed," the Count laughed. "We're here."

A door appeared in the nothing.

A door I'd unlocked but refused to enter.

"The dear girl is worried for you, Felix," he called me my name for the first and last time. "She's been kind to an old fool," St Germain chuckled. "Give her a hug for me. Time I rest," he said, waving. "I'm a little tired myself."

I turned, bidding my friend, student, and mentor farewell.

creeeeeak

"Hello, mes," I said, smiling in the silhouetting door.

"He's here!" one timekeeper screamed, wearing the first face of mine.

My second face ran, unable to speak.

The third cowered, trembling, afraid.

"After all my hard work," the fourth scowled, anger apparent. His face worn since death's door.

"Seems like," I shrugged. "Time to go."

"As you say," they echoed, "the time is yours."

Solvé

COMING BACK FROM THE dead ought to be more dramatic — like...

I dunno, trumpets in glorious fanfare at my return?

Or, unicorns prancing and bowing as I pass down a rainbow road to resettle into my body.

Better yet, I could ride in on a llama sporting a mohawk — the llama, not me — and shades — the both of us — while bluebirds shot bottle rockets at robins as tuxedoed penguins made a tasty cocktail for sipping.

But no, I just opened my eyes to the world.

And screamed. "Wait!" I cringed back from the pink-tipped gloves a stopped breath from my nose. "Nya-hah-aaa!"

"Felix!" Molly's face lit up and made to glomp.

Not wanting to die, I dodged lest the foxgloves' touch render my life fled. Ungracefully, I might add — flipping the chair over backward as I threw my feet up to keep her grabby mitts away.

"Ack," I squirmed, pointing. "Gloves off. Now."

Molly stared at me, her hands, then back to me, realizing what she still wore. Quickly she removed the green leather, entirely incongruous with her jeans and tee ensem, yet the verdant color suited her.

"But your note said..."

"I know what my note said," I said, "I wrote it — one of me did," I hedged, "and I'm saying I'm alive now again, thank you very much, unless you kill me with those, and I'd really rather not have to manifest again," I rattled off rationale faster than she could blink. I took a breath. "And I like this face."

"It's aight," Molly winked, jibe irresistible. "So, no gloves?"

I hissed, crossing my fingers in ward.

"I missed you," she laughed, eyes glistening as she waved the gloves about a bit cavalierly.

"Missed you, too, Molls," I reached to snatch the waiting death from her hands lest she touch.

"Don't call me that," she snapped, jerking the supple gloves back. Mischief split her face with a grin.

Something in her smile stirred deeper-seeded emotions — ones I thought long dead and buried. Ones I'd killed, or tried to. Molly didn't follow the snap up with a crackle or a pop, just a warm smile that spread from her grin.

"Ahem," Sassy cleared his throat. I guess he would be there — it was his house and all. "Want the room?" He hadn't shaved for a while, so his expression — simultaneously raising his eyebrows while making a kissy face — reminded me of mating caterpillars. If caterpillars mated, that is, which they don't. So maybe caterpillars fighting over a particularly tasty leaf.

"How'd you know I'd find the gloves?" Molly asked to distract from the blossoming blush reddening her face. "The note was addressed to me."

"You mean, how'd I know you'd come looking for me despite providing you a safe haven removed from time — with celestial aid, no less," I shot a look at Sassy-pants, who simply shrugged and left to give us space, "so you wouldn't, you know, wither away, while I risked my neck to figure out a way to fix what I fucked up?"

"Again with the safe BS?" Molly threw up exasperated hands, nearly hitting the lantern floating nearby — glowing bright red. "I never asked…"

"What's that?" I stopped her short. On the verge of tears at the thought of losing someone else I cared about through my own ineptitude, I nearly gave in to the darkness. Instead, I distracted myself — and Molly — pointing to her luminary companion.

"What's what?" Molly, rant derailed, turned to look — the lantern kept floating just behind her, swinging out of her view as she did.

I laughed as she chased her tail. "The little glowy thing floating there," I pointed up.

"Oh, that." Molly scooped the lantern in front of her to better look at it. "I sometimes forget it's there," she sighed. "StG made it for me," she smiled a bit sadly. "Said it worked like the one at the Last Chance," she bit her lip. "Something about the seconds of life?"

"Time spent there isn't reckoned against the seconds of one's life." I knew it well. I'd gone to a lot of trouble to leave her there for that reason.

"That's the one!" She snapped her fingers, finally clicking it into place. "Anyway, he made it so I could leave without…" She stopped, covering her mouth to hold in what she was about to say.

"Turning into a tree?" I offered, raising my eyebrow.

"How'd you?" Molly's mouth worked open and shut, eyes wide with surprise.

I smiled, trying for mysterious. I hadn't worked on my air of mystique in a while, so it was rusty. As a result, the smile came out a bit lopsided. "I knew a Trenynn once."

"Yeah you did, sugar," Sassy unhelpfully cad-called from wherever he'd gone — obviously not far out of earshot, the snoop. "I do recall saying you should find yourself a nice tree," he went on.

"Sassafras G. Hardy," I scolded, going so far as to third name him. The G stands for Grendel, by the way — a story before my time.

Molly tilted her head and giggled. "If you knew, why didn't you *say* something?"

"Forgot," I shrugged, not quite lying. "He with you?" I pointed to the luminary aloft. I wasn't sure I could face the alchemist this side of memory, but I needed to suck it up and apologize. I'd treated him terribly.

"Felix," my heart broke. "He was, but…"

"He shouldn't have been," he muttered, his face confused and a little sour. I thought they were friends?

"Why not?" He'd wanted desperately to help. "He refused to let me come alone," I fought tears.

"We didn't, ah," Felix started, scrubbing the back of his neck the way he did when skirting truths. "Part on the best terms. I need to apologize for…"

The tears won, streaming down my cheeks. I tried to speak, but my voice caught in a sob.

"Molly?"

"He's gone," I tried to say, coming out more like 'ee's hon' between the wracking heaves.

Felix's eyes filled with concern, coming to my side, unable to understand my tear-stained words. It was too much. First,

Felix was dead — I thought, alive again now — then St Germain slipped away to the corruption. *How the hell does an immortal die?* I wanted to scream, but there were only tears.

"It's okay, sugar pie," I heard Sassy say from the door. "Go on, let it out," he encouraged, shoving Felix closer so I could hug him.

To his credit, Felix did let me hug him, even hugged me back a little — though he was entirely too tense about it, and then he ruined it. "Someone fill me in?"

I sobbed again, trying to form the thoughts.

"Your alchemist friend is no longer with us," Sassy translated. "Clawed his way to you, and gave out. Departing this plane."

I felt Felix go rigid.

"Where?" All warmth and humor left as he spoke — his voice unlike I'd ever heard it. Startled by the sudden chill, I shied away. Sassy frowned at his resumed callous.

"After he passed, I laid him in here," the big guy said, motioning for Felix and me to follow.

It'd been horrible — the two of them splayed motionless, clutching the brass clock. I'd crumbled, defeated in my quest — everything I'd worked for had come crashing down around my ears.

I guess I don't really know how it was supposed to have gone, but not like that. Then, though his heart wasn't beating, I swear I saw Felix twitch.

Gently, I'd tried to pull the dead alchemist away, but he wouldn't budge. "Help me!" The corruption was still spreading, contaminating his remains, and I worried it'd infect Felix, too.

Sassy, irresistible as an avalanche, pulled St Germain away — wrapping him delicately in a thick blanket and carrying him to where the big man now led us.

The room was dark, save for my lantern's light glowing blue again. It did that whenever the corruption was near. My stomach turned, thinking of it consuming that dear old man.

"He only spoke well of you," I said of a sudden. "Never a bad word, only concern." I brushed hair back from my eyes, looking up at Felix, his face stone. "And admiration, I think. However you parted, whatever came between, he was proud of you."

Felix didn't reply, merely walked forward to pull back the blanket.

I wish he hadn't. The poor Count's face, blighted and riddled with throbbing black decay — vacant eyes unmoving. I looked away.

"Where's his earring? The diamond stud," Felix finally said, a touch hollow. How could he think about diamonds when his friend lay there dead? But since he mentioned it.

"He hasn't worn it since we left the bar," I said. I thought that was the last I saw it, at any rate.

Felix let his eyes go distant, apparently lost in thought. Briefly, they fluttered between the absent earring and the flickering light hovering just over my head.

"Felix?" I shifted, uncomfortable in the silence. I've never much liked silence since I could talk. Sassy'd declined to join us in the room, and Felix certainly wasn't helping, so it was far too quiet. "He was immortal, right?" I opened my mouth and let words tumble out. "Kept saying he was an alchemist and had been alive since before the French Revolution and that he knew *you* way back then and really lots of things I couldn't believe."

"He tended to say lots of things," Felix said. Neither confirmation nor denial. "In too many words."

I laughed.

"I even started believing him," I went on. "Showed me some marvelous things. Made me this lantern, had this wicked cool cigarette case with an infinity match, even played Hank's fiddle when things got bad. It was moving," I sighed, remembering the golden afterglow of the attack on the bar.

That Felix raised an eyebrow at. "Certainly was an accomplished musician." I knew there had to be more to it, but I'd ask another time.

"So, I mean, taking all that into account," it was my turn to prevaricate, "if he was so immortal, how can he die?"

It was a good question — one I'd been puzzling over since the bombshell dropped. St Germain *shouldn't* have been able to die. Not unless...

"He ran out of time," I said, coming to the only conclusion I could.

That his diamond was gone was the biggest clue. I'd never had it straight from him, but I could draw my own conclusions. *That* was where he'd hidden his hour's pay. It had to be.

Molly looked a bit puzzled. And as good as she was at them, she didn't have all the pieces to this one just yet.

"How much did he tell you about his immortality?" The alchemist's secrets bled into my own. Some of them I wasn't ready to share. Not even with Molly.

"Just that he was," she counted off, "and that was all he said, but he kept drinking something from a flask when he thought no one was really paying attention, so I figured that had something to do with it."

"Something like that," I interjected.

"I saw him shoot it right before we jumped in the T-bird — did you know it can drive itself? Has a mouth on him, too," she side-tracked. I'd wondered how they made it to Sassy's.

"Lenny's not much for people these days."

"Lenny… nevermind. So when we saw you dead, I begged him for something, and he said he was out."

Ah.

I reached up and gently took hold of the luminary ever floating behind Molly, pulling it down to look at the crafting. St Germain's handiwork, to be sure. Pooled inside the vial the wick drew from, I saw what should have kept the alchemist alive.

I couldn't tell her that part, so I lied. Just a little.

"I think he traded his life for mine." It wasn't exactly untrue, just slightly removed. "I saw him, you know," I said. "Just before I woke up. Said it was time to come back."

I sent the lantern to float back over her head, keeping her safe.

Silently I thanked my friend for protecting her. And promised I'd see him again.

"Sassy-pants?" I knew he was lurking just outside. He'd given us our privacy again, but I felt certain he sure as hell wasn't going to leave either of us alone.

"Yes, hon?"

"Can you do me a favor?" I put on my most winningest smile, nodding back toward my friend.

"How many times do I have to remind you," the Bigfoot sighed, overly dramatic. "This is *not* Sassy's Self-Storage," he pouted.

I pouted right back, going so far as to bat my eyelashes.

"Fine." He threw his hands up in defeat.

He'd given up just shy of my 'Pretty please.' I was pulling out the big guns for this one.

The immortal alchemist, the Count of St Germain, deserved at least that much.

Sunshine warmed my face as I sat rocking on the lowest porch of the pagoda. I luxuriated in the rays, watching as they slowly dipped between the teeth of the mountains, disappearing until the new day's dawn.

My breath still, time stretched on as I felt the earth beckon my feet — enticing me to dip my roots in its rich soil. Homey and inviting. I saw why Sassy called this place his sanctuary.

"Molly?" Distant.

A hand on my shoulder. I jerked from my reverie.

"Molly?" Felix, concern filled his face as I puzzled. "Molly!" He squeezed my shoulder three times, fixing me back to reality.

The brightness dimmed to faint afterglow as darkness settled in, blanketing the valley in shadow. Warmth behind me reflected in Felix's eyes as my luminary companion returned. He'd borrowed it for...something I forgot.

"Hmmm," I stretched, limbering stiff legs. I wiggled my toes — yes, I did have toes, not roots.

"Good morning, sunshine," he smiled, "have a nice nap?"

"Did I nap?" I hadn't felt it. The sun was just so relaxing, I lost myself in the memory of...

SNAP

"Stay with me," Felix sought my attention. "Spring is upon us, no longer winter's rest."

Rest sounded good. Yes, I wanted more. I was so tired. It *had* been a very long winter, and I'd yet to take a nap. But...that wasn't right. I never took naps. Not in winter, not ever.

I spent winters with Elder, deep in the snow. With birds nestling among my prickly leaves and eating from my hands. Winters were grand, when people didn't cut me. Elder'd been so kind, keeping me company. Talking to me of the world beyond the woods.

Music. Faint trills of it drifting to my ears. Flowers bloomed in my mind, so many fields bursting with color. I breathed it all in — the sweet warmth of new growth bursting to life. Fire kindled inside, sparking anew.

It was time to awake.

Felix, sweet Felix, leaned against the porch rail, watching me rock as he played mellifluous music on the flute now put to his lips. His fingers danced gracefully as the birds sang in his song. Brooks babbled their secrets, free now from the freeze to gossip. Redolent notes of spring's promise renewed.

Vibrant peace.

Shattered by a rock. One, I think, thrown at my head — but not reached.

"A kindness if ye please," I heard the Bloodybell hiss from beyond the dark. He spoke the words of form, not truly intending them. One must abide custom, though.

Felix's hand bled around the jagged rock he'd clutched lightning quick from the air, a single drop falling to the rail on which he leaned.

"A kindness if ye please," Bill o'deSoul repeated, tinged now with murderous glee. "Since ye've accepted my given gift with such gracious alacrity." He stalked closer, appearing just at the edge of the light spilling from the house.

"When will you learn to simply leave me be?" Another drop dripped as Felix clenched the rock tighter. Calm though his voice seemed, I knew him enough to tell he wrestled with anger beneath.

"Bill!" I snapped, my peaceful serenade ruined. "What's the big idea? You're breaking our deal!" Felix looked sharply at that. I guess he hadn't read all his texts.

"Not so, not so," the murder-hobo waved dismissive claws. "No harm came to you, nor would, I wagered since *he* stood between."

"What if he'd missed? Huh? What then?" I started into the dark to give him a piece of my mind. Felix's hand stopped me at the rail.

"*He* wouldn't," Bill tittered. "No, not *him*," he spat. "*He can't.*"

"What *deal* did you make with the goblin?"

"Oh, well," I stepped lightly around the topic. "So, um."

"Your charlatan heart," the Bloodybell leapt closer, cackling.

"A *chance* at..." I tried to correct, but Bill's mouth ran on.

"For my most helpful aid," he held clawed hand to chest in feigned humble air.

"StG and Hank said..." I continued my defense.

"With which to find you. And now here you are," his broken bone smile cracked his gnarled face.

"Yes," Felix said, danger lighting in his eyes. "Here I am," he turned and smiled, arms spreading wide.

He flicked his wrist, stone twisting in bloodied hand as he strode off the porch and into the shadowed dark. A gold coin appeared in the twisted stone's place, smeared now with blood, I could see, as he held it up into the light.

"A kindness for you," Felix said in a tone. "For your troubles and your aid, most needed, I can see…" he drew out, "…for a time." He flicked the coin at Bill, who dove to catch. "But no more," his voice froze cold, appearing next to the grubbing Bloodybell faster than a blink — boot firmly planted on the squirming killer's back.

"Enough of your games, goblin," he spat as Bill struggled. Fireflies sprang up from the flailed grass, lighting the night in eerie protest.

"Felix!" I'd never seen him like this. I'd heard and hazarded guesses, but never seen. "Don't kill him!" Never did I think I'd have to say such a phrase — not to him. "He doesn't deserve it."

"Doesn't he?" Felix's head jerked up, words harsher than I ever heard from him, then he softened. "Doesn't he," he repeated, a bit unsure.

"Whatever his sins, no," I said gently. "Because then they become yours, and he cannot atone."

Felix took a deep breath and sighed, shutting his eyes.

"We'll have a reckoning, you and I," Felix said, raising his grinding boot. "But not this day nor the next."

"Pox, plague, and blight be," Bill spat, jumping to a crouch — his goat-slit eyes staring hard.

"Eilean a' Chombraidh. One year hence," Felix formally intoned. "I'll bring the booze." The smile that followed was up to no good.

"On yer house and thee!" Bill ignored Felix's offer and kept cursing.

"None of that now," I chided the willful goat-man. "You got your chance, I'd say," I smiled, turning his own kind of words upon him. "That you did not make the most of it is no fault of mine."

"Begone, Bill o'deSoul," Felix said, exasperated. "You've your kindness in blood and gold."

"My chance is not up yet," he scowled and lunged.

"You are not welcome here," Felix clapped his hands, disappearing the murder-hobo mid-strike.

"What'd you do to him!?" Molly demanded, hand on hip.

"He's fine," I assured her. "Just no longer in our hair." Or the Sanctuary. For which he should be grateful. He'd apparently earned enough of a reprieve from Molly that I'd be remiss utilizing more drastic measures, but I damn well didn't have time for the volatile vermin. How many lives must he plague me?

I pushed thoughts of the Bloodybell from my head. He could wait. I had more pressing concerns.

"How..."

"Feeling better?" I didn't even let her go down that path — we had other places to be. "Thank you for letting me borrow the luminary. I'm sorry I took it so long." It'd been enlightening — heh, get it? — what the alchemist had concocted with what I assume was the last of his elixir. *That* recipe he hadn't shared, even with me — though I knew the main component: time.

"I am, actually." She turned slightly inward in examination. Her usual pep and spunk had diminished ever so slightly to my eyes. "Where'd you learn to play like that?"

Shivers seemed to run up her spine at the blissful thought. Now that I knew, she reminded me so much of "Hazel," I said, naming my Trenynn tryst.

"Little on the nose," Molly's face scrinched. "I know names don't mean much to you," she was wrong, "but you really ought to learn people's," she said. "It's only polite."

"That's the name she gave," I defended, slightly prickled. "And names mean a great deal to me. That's why I give out so many." If only people wore their proper name-tags, I wouldn't have to fix them in place so much. I sighed, not getting into it — but it was a chore and a half!

The look she shot let me know my cryptic game was still on point. Good. Let her guess.

"Besides, you're one to talk, *Molly*," extra emphasis on the M. I raised my eyebrow to add even more. She'd only changed one letter. Lazy.

"Does *everyone* know?" she sighed. "Anyway," dropping it, "did it work?"

"I don't know," I said, frankly unsure if my contraption would. "I got the job done, sure." It hadn't been easy — it's surprisingly hard to return a piece of the infinite. Not to mention the fact that I didn't have half the Count's artificing skill, but seeing as he was currently unavailable, I'd done my best. "But I don't know if it worked. We'll just have to wait and see."

We looked in on the prone Count's remains, lit now by a wan light glowing mottled blue and red. I'd devised a lantern of my own — more glorified candleholder than true luminary. It certainly didn't float all fancy like his, but it didn't need to — just keep St Germain's corruption at bay long enough for...

What, I wasn't sure. I had my suspicions the alchemist still had a trick up his autotelic sleeves.

"Do we have time for that?" Molly looked up at her O-StG model, floating dutifully by her side. Its light had grown dimmer from the bits I'd extricated to craft the spare.

"No, not really. Clock's ticking," as it ever does, but more so now. Originally, she had enough elixir fueling the luminary for another couple days or so, I'd wager, but now it was scant less than one. "We need to get you back."

"Yay," she certainly didn't enthuse. "Do we have to?"

"I mean," I shrugged, "if you wanna put down some roots and sleep it off for the next century, nah." I knew now Molly'd eventually be fine; she just wasn't used to the ginger fairy's kiss — being of the evergreen Trenynn who had a long-standing pact. I really didn't want to think about the fallout from *that* particular breach of conduct.

She frowned, thinking about it until her phone buzzed.

"What have I gotten myself into," I muttered under my breath.

The call had been from Hank, except not really. He'd butt-dialed or something. The concerning part was the voice I'd overheard on the other end.

Deirdre. Her sweet self-assured positivity positively ground my gears now that I knew it was all faked. I mean, they usually are — those streamers — but I'd seen her true face in the fog.

And I'd left her to ingratiate herself in *my* bar with the friends I hold dearest.

That was the only reason I'd agreed to Felix's plan.

No, it's not a plan. It's stupid. It's madness.

"Well, I have been cooped up in a clock for the last few months binge-watching reruns of *This is Your Life*," he laughed. "Some screws are bound to come loose!" Oops, guess I said that last part out loud.

"Shouldn't we have driven?" Now that I knew the Thunderbird was inhabited by a deific creature — smart-mouthed as he was — it seemed a really good idea to have him along for backup. Plus, I was tired of walking.

"Nah, get lost faster this way." Felix turned and walked backward, sidestepping roots and snagging branches despite the unwieldy bundle he carried. How? I'm a fucking tree, and I can't even do it that effortlessly. "You still got the gloves?"

Of course I had the gloves, I didn't bother to say. My face alone said it was a stupid question. They were safely tucked in the twist. I really didn't like carrying them after he explained their soul-stealing capabilities. That part had been left out of the note.

"Just checking." He turned back around, traipsing along no path.

Paths meant people. Paths meant maps and known routes. The fastest way back to the Last Chance was to be well and truly lost, and those things precluded that happening. He'd even made me turn my phone off. I shuddered in the digital dark.

"It's not like she's going to let us just walk in," I'd objected to his lunacy. "The bar was under siege for days," I filled him in on the attacks. "Nothing could get through. Had to sneak out through the *secret tunnel*," I couldn't help but sing. Damn earworms.

"Not so secret," he said. "And Deirdre walked in," he added. "So can we."

"She came in before the attacks," I argued.

"Did she?"

I thought back. *No*, the attacks came with *her*.

"She put you in danger to draw me out," Felix said. "Didn't work. I was done adrift by then."

"We noticed," I surled. Read your damn texts!

"Then she used you as a stalking horse to find me where I wasn't," he malapropped, I think. That one's always confused me.

"So?"

"So why would she keep laying siege to a place neither you nor I were?"

He had a point. Hank's butt-dial hadn't seemed agitated or anxious. In fact, the entire scene sounded jovial and lively. Glasses clinked, drunks cheered, I thought I even heard myself singing karaoke in the background — damnit Maya.

Neon flickered in the distance as we remained unaccosted.

"What'd I tell you?" It was mildly infuriating when he was so right.

"Lots of things, so what?" I smarmed. "Still a stupid idea." I wouldn't let him have it.

"Halt!" One spear pointed through the brush.

"Who goes?" A mallet raised, silhouetted in neon.

"You lumps, it's Molly!" The third gnome wrangled his brothers.

I giggled, grabbing Bert up for a hug.

"Friends of yours?" Felix eyed the armed fjøsnisser warily.

"What's it to ya?" Snorkir hopped on Cypnir — or was it Cypnir on Snorkir — straining to reach Felix's eye level without their top brother Bert. "Huh? This bum bothering you," the tower of gnomes turned.

"Guys, *this* is Felix," I said, putting Bert down so I could introduce them all.

"Hrng," Bert hrnged, unimpressed. "Don't seem worth the fuss."

"Probably not," Felix laughed and shrugged.

"You two alone, Miss Molly?" Cypnir, I think, raised an eyebrow. "Still not safe," he slung his mallet over his shoulder.

"Yeah, where's the Count?" Snorkir, by process of elimination, asked.

I misted up a bit. "St Germain's..."

"Unavoidably detained," Felix finished, subtly shaking his head.

"And the bumper?" Bert referred to Bill.

"Bumped off," Felix flashed a toothy smile.

"Good riddance," the fjøsnisser spat in unison.

"Still not safe, you said," I drew the conversation back. "But you're out patrolling?"

"Oh." Bert puffed out his chest, leading us up to the door. "Safe enough with us thumping bumpers." The brothers each put on their most menacing face. It was kind of cute.

"Been pretty quiet since," Cypnir mimed me, leaving through the no-longer-secret tunnel.

"Feeeeelixxxx!!!" Maya-me split the night with a scream and ran from the entrance, launching herself into his arms — knocking his brown-wrapped bundle loose in the process.

Her legs locked around him — in too-tight leather pants I'd never wear and a top...I needed to have a word with my double. Before I could say that word, though, she grabbed hold of his hair and kissed him with my face.

And from the looks of it, my tongue. I blushed.

A half-step behind, my shadow lashed out — wrapping around Maya-me's limbs and prying her free from Felix to dangle in the air.

"Let me go," she struggled, whining with my voice.

"Um." A stunned Felix looked between the pair of us, not sure what to say.

"Ah-a," Hank doddered in the door. "He's back," he called inside. "Well, come on, old son," he waved. "We been waitin'."

et Coagule

LOOK, BAD THINGS HAPPEN — always do and always are going to. But there's an after. And that's the important part — something I'm getting the hang of.

The part where you pick up the pieces and put them back together again in whatever shape they may take.

It won't be the same. It'll never be the same again, but it will *be* and that's something you can work with. That's one of the things my formerly-immortal friend taught me as a fundamental principle of alchemy — solvé et coagule.

Latin — probably — for 'break apart and put back together again as something new.' And if there's a better analogy for whatever Hell I just went through, I don't know it.

Deirdre *was* waiting for us when we got back to the Last Chance. But I'll get to that in a second — she didn't pounce as soon as we walked in — I was distracted by Hank.

I didn't know how the old devil's words would hit me. I knew all the ones he'd spoken before — relived them and recalled them — but these were fresh and new. Unheard.

For the first time in a long stretch, I didn't know what came next — and I felt entirely ill at ease.

The history between us slammed home. The good, the fractious. All the hours spent dicing and betting. Beating the devil to keep my soul and win my love.

"Good seein' ya, old son," Hank gripped my shoulder with his gnarled hand — risking whatever backlash may befall him. I reflexively pulled back lest it do just that, but he held firm — grip like iron.

"I'm sorry, Hank," I straightened, looking him gently in the eye. "I fucked it all up." Tears welled up.

"Ya did," Hank grumbled. "Damn hothead."

"You'd know," I winked. The old devil split a smile, wicked and wide. "Time to make it right," I added, low and under my breath, stepping closer to squeeze his shoulder in a half-hug.

Fire lit in his eyes unlike I'd seen outside of memory.

"Ya don't say, ha?" He cocked his head askance and squinted at me.

"Let me get you a drink." I walked him to the bar. "Rakozy said you let him fiddle a bit..." I trailed off in conspiracy.

I sat in the corner of Beckett's, scribbling my thoughts as I watched Damian throw down with Sassy — shots vs rocks. One shot glass for Damian, one rocks glass for Sassy-pants — had to keep it fair. My liver cringed at the abuse.

So did my wallet — Damian was paying. Eeesh. Was much easier holding up bootleggers for their booze, but they weren't running rum anymore since it was all legal-like.

"Bullshit." Damian wiped his mouth, turning over the shot glass. "You're so full of it, Felix, it's leaking out of your ears."

I was, usually.

"That's what happened." I shrugged and smiled. Mischief danced in my eyes.

"First off," Damian turned toward me as the bartender poured up another round."I don't believe for a second you just walked in that place all hunky-dory." I waved the drink off, having had enough for the moment. *I* wasn't keeping up with those two, not tonight.

"It's a trap," I Ackbarred — shaking my face in imitation of the admiral.

"Second," he smirked, but not to be interrupted, "can I meet Elvis?" He turned to a belching Sassy-pants.

"Ooh hoo-hoo ho," he covered his mouth. "How uncivilized," he belched again, refocusing on Damian. "Sure, hon," he smiled, "if you karaoke with me!"

Sassy slid off the stool, standing even taller in heels and sashaying up to the stage — all dolled up for his night out. Damian threw back an extra shot of liquid courage — or stupidity — throwing me a look before heading up to the stage.

Karaoke night at Beckett's. Joy. The DJ cued up the next song and the opening beats of "Under Pressure" thrummed out of the speakers. Maybe I'd need that drink after all — Sassy was in a singing mood.

Now, you'll not hear me tell the Bigfoot he can't carry a tune even with all those bootleg bourbon barrels he keeps stashed around. Nope. Nuh-uh.

But someone should.

All that mattered was that he enjoyed himself and I had earplugs — which I put in as he strut the stage.

I couldn't blame Damian — the whole thing was far-fetched — but still. Stranger things have happened. I'd learned that for sure during my jog down memory lane. Still coming to grips with a lot of it, quite honestly.

"There you are," Molly found me — smiling as she slid up on the stool next to me. I think that's what she said anyway. Good earplugs, sadly removed.

"Here I am," I confirmed, screwing the cap on my fountain pen. Molly tried to peek over my pages as I folded the journal shut. "Spoilers," I teased.

She pouted briefly, then moved on. "I've been looking for you."

"Did you find me?" Best cryptic face — on.

She pondered a moment, tasting the words for tricks.

"I think I may have," she decided, brushing back her now-black hair — a flirty smile spread across her face. I still wasn't sure how to take that.

"Needed a change of scenery," I evaded, leaving out that I was hiding. Things had gotten, well, *complicated*. I'd hoped the karaoke would prove a buffer, but here she was.

"Quite the scenery." She twisted to see Sassy-pants go for round two with some on-the-nose Aerosmith. Yea-ah.

"Bet he wore the heels just to sing that one." I whistled at the appropriate parts.

"Doesn't explain the top hat, though," she observed. It didn't.

"Maybe he just felt extra fancy tonight," I cheered. "I thought you didn't like karaoke," I turned the topic back to her. "Otherwise, I'd have invited you," I lied. Politely.

"Molly-kins, mi amour," Damian slid up beside, all sung out. "What're you having?" He waved another bill at the bartender.

"Chardonnay," she smiled. Since when? And Molly-kins? She hated nicknames. Was a stabbing affront.

"You heard the lady." Damian ordered another round of whiskies for himself and Sassy. I knocked back mine and joined in. "Now," he turned back to us, "Felix has been telling some tales I think too tall," he eyed.

"Has he now?" Her lips curled in a petite smile. "What makes you think that? Felix would *never* lie," sarcasm dripped from the laugh that followed.

"For starters," Damian motioned to her hair, "your hair is not white."

"Well, it's not *now*," she laughed. "I changed it up." Her mischievous smile grew wide behind her newly arrived wine.

Everything changes.

Preempting a *pics or it didn't happen*, I took out my phone — flicking through. "See?" I showed him the white hair.

"Well damn, you look hot," he flirted, drunk and grabbing at my phone to see through blurred eyes. I never let it go, even as he pulled it closer to see, pinching to zoom. "I know that moose!"

"He tell you I was a tree, too?" I toed the line.

"Yeah!" He got too close, examining. "Are you?" He looked for leaves.

"Not a tree," I didn't lie, precisely. Felix sighed.

"How gullible do you think I am?" Damian listed toward Felix. "You made it all up!"

"You're drinking with Bigfoot," Felix reminded him, tossing back his Scotch.

I didn't think Damian would last much longer, honestly. Probably wouldn't remember much — or think he was hallucinating — so I threw Felix a bone.

A crown of leaves circled my head — sharp and green-mottled-white with red berries — growing and fading in an instant. One sprig fell into Damian's drink. "Not a *tree*," I emphasized, winking and moving on to my second Chardonnay.

Damian's mouth dropped open. "Holy..."

"Missing an L there, chief," Felix threw in.

"Molly!" Sassy-pants squeed, joining us from the stage. "Girl, you look ravishing!" I did, not that *someone* had said anything. I knew he noticed; he notices *everything* he doesn't say. The not saying irked.

"Damn Sassy," I sought a compliment, "you got some pipes! And I *love* the heels." I ignored the top hat for the time being — slightly offended as a perpetually short person. Sassy was tall enough, damnit.

"Where on earth d'you find the size forty-five clodhoppers?" Felix slurred his words.

"Rude!" I scolded. The pumps were fab, stylish. He was drunk. Rather, acting drunk — I was pretty sure. What was he up to?

"Those charming little cobblers you recommended," Sassy smooched. "Magic, those two."

Felix toasted his empty, feigning confusion as he downed air.

"I think we should get you home, love," I took Felix by the hand. He stiffened at my slip. "Damian," I carried on despite, making our exit, "always a pleasure. Sassy," I smiled, "shopping Sunday? I'd love to meet these cobblers." Felix stumbled behind me, carrying on the inebriation.

"Get your passport ready, sugar." Sassy re-engaged Damian in the battle of livers, doubling up what he'd missed singing.

Felix dutifully leaned on me as we swayed through the crowd, acting as part of the escape. I relished in the warmth of his touch, so familiar now. Except.

"Sorry," he pulled away. "You didn't need to," he waved his fingers, "you know." Ah. Still stupidly protective.

"Just getting out before Sassy-pants tried to get *me* up there," I laughed, pulling back my hair. Notice, damnit! "Thanks for the save," I sparkled at him.

"How about some psychogeography?"

"Is that safe?" I mocked him, openly. Feigning fright at the night.

"Naturally not so much, but it's fun," he swept a bow. "Pick a rule."

"What kind of rule?" My heart warmed. This was more like my Felix.

"Something like turning left when you spot a certain color," he jumped up on a bench, "or following a cat," he shaded his eyes and looked around. "No cats." He jumped down, slightly disappointed.

"How 'bout dragons?"

"None of those either," he smiled. Asshole'd known Elliot was a dragon and never said a word. "C'mon, pick."

He was trying hard to distract me. I guess we weren't going to talk about it. Whatever'd started growing between us. "Okay," I played along. "Whenever..."

Bzzbzzzz.

I was stopped before I could start.

"So which is it?" I asked a random nurse passerby.

"Excuse me?" Perplexed, but I had her attention.

"The sign." I hooked my thumb over my shoulder at the one taped to the vending machine.

Confusion clouded her eyes, warring with concern that I'd escaped the psych ward.

"That sign has someone's name mentally appended — unlike Emmett's —" I recalled the propane prohibition at the Stony Meadows Punkin Chunkin that explicitly threw shade. "So, I figure it has a story behind it."

"Um," the nurse drew a blank as to what I was asking.

"I figure," I went on, "some hotshot doctor is being funny, using the endoscope claw to grab midnight snacks." The sign in question had a Ghostbusters circle-slash over surgical equipment. "But then," I leaned against the machine, "you'd know who it was and just tell the fictitious Dr. Shmee to cut it out."

The kind nurse let me prattle — her bedside manner excellent. Maybe she was used to dealing with rambly old men — like me. Didn't look it with this face, but I was.

"My money is on the janitor, though." I waggled my eyebrows conspiratorially. She giggled.

"The janitor? You mean sweet Mr. Steve?"

Oooh, I had a name now. A real one. Likely one belonging on a handy-dandy nametag.

"Yes, exactly!" The story started spinning. "You see, Mr. Steve has been running machinery like that his entire life and has almost a savantness about him. Added to that, they make these things so easy to operate now, anyone who can run a claw machine can perform surgery." I patted the vending machine, which precipitously dropped a precariously perched bag of cashews. "Score!"

I handed the blue sea-salted goodness to the young nurse.

"Mr. Steve would never steal," she assured me. "Unlike some…" Her look stabbed me accusatorially.

"Oh! But that's the twist," I countered. "He did, but for the children."

"What children?" By now, the nurse had crossed her arms and was rather visibly tired of my antics.

"The sick kids he nicks the snacks for in the middle of the night." My eyes sparkled with mischief. Everyone loves a sob. A right heart tugging tear-jerker.

"There you are, Felix," Molly found me.

Off the hook, the nurse made busy her escape. "How's she doing?"

Molly's phone had interrupted the little game of distraction I'd begun playing, letting her know that Deirdre was finally awake. Poor girl.

Last time I'd seen her — awake, that is — she'd been crying blood. Hell of a thing and all kinds of messed up.

Despite Molly's texted declaration, the seer hadn't been a baddie at all, just a patsy. A cat's paw. Dupe. Pawn. Chump. Sucker. Whatever synonym you wanted to throw at her — she was a victim. Caught up in a struggle centuries in the making.

My bloody mess.

Deirdre *had* been waiting for us at the Last Chance, like I said, but not exactly for nefarious reasons — which I'd figured out *after* we'd cornered her. Hank, myself, and Molly, with Elder blocking the door.

Let me rewind.

"Guys," Deirdre'd brightened as we came to her back room. I think she'd been streaming. "I'm so glad to see you back safe," she rose, taking Molly by the hand.

Play it cool, I'd advised her. *We don't know how things are shaking out. Best not to trip any traps.* There'd been no overt threat that I could see. Quite the opposite, which was hella confusing.

Hank and I'd shared our drinks and conspiracy while Molly'd caught up with Elder and the others — each wanted a bit of her attention. Now it was time to see the reader.

"I hear I have you to thank for setting her path," I stood next to Molly as Hank leaned next to the door, waiting.

"I only relay the guide's messages." As always, Deirdre radiated positivity. "But I'm quite glad they got through." Her eyes went distant, staring at my aura as she had at Halloween. Her face twisted and fear clouded her eyes. "What..." Her voice fell silent — the room dimmed dark.

"Finally, you come before me," a voice neither Deirdre's nor Zestra's came from the seer's throat. Gone were the lovely emeralds and willowy hazel eyes, replaced instead by a green putrid and festering — the sickly color of fresh pressed olives.

"Only polite," I smarmed. "You've been taking such good care of my friends." I strode forward, menacingly.

"Nah-ah," Deirdre's sharp-nailed finger waved, putrid eyes locked on me. Good. Focus on me, you prick.

I stopped, playing along. "Release her," I ordered. "You want me, we can talk elsewhere — no medium necessary." If I'd been myself, I'd have seen it ages ago — she was possessed.

Risk of the family business, it seemed. I recalled Zestra having some issues she'd needed help with from time to time.

"I think not," the spirit cackled. "This vessel suits me just fine."

I shrugged and smiled. I'd asked nicely.

Right on cue, Hank stepped from the deepened dark — pulling fiddle from case, bathing the room with its heavenly light. Gone was the stoop to his back, the crook to his wrist. The old devil rose to his former full height and rosined up his bow.

Now, fire didn't exactly flow from his fingertips, but rays of gold certainly did — spearing at the darkness, driving it away. Filth manifest boiled from Deirdre like black flame, her body going rigid — tears of blood in her stricken eyes.

The twisted *thing* I'd seen spring from the slain preacher-man that day in the cave rose higher, filling the room with foul presence. The very air felt corrupt in my lungs as I tried not to breathe it in. My sin given shape.

"Now!"

Molly, too, had been lurking in the shadows, preparing her part as I'd played distraction. I'd hated that I was ultimately useless against such esoteric threats — the physical much more my specialty — but I was no longer alone.

Green-gloved hands reached for Deirdre but stopped short, pulling at the putrescence wherever the pink tips brushed — tearing it asunder. Thank goodness Molly'd picked up on my hints — there was already enough blood on my hands. I hated staining hers as well. But she'd insisted — stubborn.

The foxgloves were the stuff of aether — able to manipulate the fabric of life itself, if one were of the right persuasion. Death to the living, and life to the dead. They hadn't worked for me then as they worked for her now — but at a cost.

Everything a price.

Deirdre collapsed, torn free of the invading souls as Hank played on. The shadows danced in the holy light, writhing and bucking in Molly's gloved grip as it burned away the filth. Pain and agony ripped tears from my eyes, knowing my Dena had been mired in this for so long. I clenched my fist hard, waiting.

I saw it — the faintest glimmer — and took my chance.

Fool's key in hand, I closed my eyes and did what I do best.

I cheated, returning a piece to the infinite.

Felix had twisted the key he held and the world went white — I mean, it was already pretty damn bright, with Hank sawing at his golden fiddle filling the room with the heavenly rays, but this was different.

I felt floaty. Adrift.

Pretty nice, actually.

"So, you're the minx who caught my husband's eye, huh?" A woman appeared behind me, I think — direction was somewhat meaningless at that moment, but it felt like she was behind me and to the left.

"I suppose it depends on who your husband is and who you are." I tried to spin toward the voice but drifted lazily in a small circle instead.

"The reckless fool out there with the key," the lithe woman sighed, smiling as she sat at an easel, painting the world that wasn't. Slowly the empty white spaces filled in with the strokes of her brush. "And I'm Dena," Felix's wife spared a glance my way. Dazzling and mischievous all at once.

"So, it worked?" The plan had been out of my wheelhouse — souls and fiddles and demon possession and a touch of exorcism. All I knew was I needed to grab hold of whatever came out of Deirdre with the gloves and hang on.

Twinkles grew in her eyes as the river scene reflected stars in a night sky, now. "You could say that." Dena set her brush down and rose, dusting off her britches and stretching. "Thank you," she hugged me.

"You're welcome?" I wasn't sure what I'd done.

"And that's what makes you special," Dena smiled at me, her gaze distant and unsettlingly knowing. *Are you reading my mind?* I thought as a test.

"No, I'm not reading your mind," Dena laughed. "That was a gimme," she winked, "as Felix would say."

"So what then?"

"You do the right thing without knowing exactly what you do," Dena explained. "You create possibilities, like I used to."

"Used to?"

"Why yes, Molly, I'm dead now," Dena deadpanned. "Didn't you get the memo?" Her wide eyes gently stared through me.

"But..."

"A memory of a memory," she said before I could get my thoughts straight.

Are you sure you're not psychic?

"Nothing more," she didn't rise to that one. "But I can rest a bit easier knowing someone like you is with him. He needs it even if he doesn't know." Sadness crept in. Love tinged slightly bitter.

"He blames himself," I said before I could think. "Misses you."

"Always does," Dena sighed. "Blames himself for you, too," she ran her fingers through my white hair — scar of the ginger fairy's kiss.

"Not his fault," I grimaced.

"Never learns." Where Dena's fingers touched, my hair grew black. I felt the void growing more whole again. "But it's time for us both to go," she faded. "Take care..."

"I can totally see it," Deirdre said from her hospital bed. Radiantly positive as always, her eyes flickered through my aura — or something like that. "Can feel her with you now, a bit," she focused.

I ran my hand through my hair, no longer bleached pale. Doubts and confusion filled my mind. I was having a hard time separating my emotions.

"She helped me, too," Deirdre teared up. First crack I'd seen in her demeanor. "When I was..." she trailed off.

Possessed, I shuddered at the thought. The things she'd been made to do.

"Only reason I made it," the seer struggled with words. I handed her a fresh cup of tea, sadly no Irish — doctor's orders.

"Me too, I think."

The painting sits dim now on the wall, unmoving. Like any other painting, really — some guy sitting on a giant stone statue head in the middle of a pond, fishing beneath a tree.

Whatever was left of my Dena — the bit of her soul she'd imbued in the wedding gift — gone. Fed to the foxgloves — sacrifice. Everything a price.

But it worked. That's what mattered.

It'd been close, but until I lose, I can always win.

"Are you done yet?" Molly derailed my thought, poking her head through the doorway. Her raven hair cascaded in waves as she leaned in.

I think the gloves had something to do with that, too. Regaining something the ginger fairy's kiss had stripped away, perhaps. You'd have to ask her. But she's no longer stuck in the lantern's light.

Her shadow stretched out ahead, impatient as ever, taking the pen from my hand and shutting my notebook as she hopped up on the desk. Stuck or not, she still owns the Last Chance. Lets Hank run it, though.

"Just finishing," I lied — there was so much more to say.

"Good," she barely waited for my response. "I want to try out that crazy map thing," she fought for the words.

"Psychogeography?"

"That's the one!" Her eyes sparkled, hungry for more adventure.

I looked up at the old bronze clock, sitting on a shelf next to the painting. It, too, had changed — the dials and all were the same. One side still graven with the Wheel of Fortune, but now — in place of the Fool gripping the key stood the Magician manifest.

"Sure, why not?"

I still had time.

Next Up

Felix's adventures continue in *Off Chance*

Also By

Felixverse
Felix Chance
Second Chance
Off Chance

Science Fiction
Pandora Squad

Anthologies
"Into the Fire" in *Hidden Villains Arise*
"The Iron Sigh" in *Behind the Shadows*

Humor
98 Rabbits: An Assemblage of Words

Sign Up

Want the latest and greatest about all my wonderful words?

Just visit: halfacrepond.com/newsletter/

My Thanks

THANK YOU FOR DIVING in to the world of Felix Chance. I hope I have entertained you with my words. If I have, please rate and leave a kind word or two so others may find their way to these pages.

About

j.e. pittman is an emerging author dabbling in many speculative worlds. He blurs the borders between genre and crafts salient lies to tell a measure of truth. His work has been described as: capriciously chimeric, dreamlike, and a vivid enigma with indelible images stamped on your brain. Discover more of his words on www.halfacrepond.com